I0608524

Shameful Shadows

Ditta Sylvester

LMH PUBLISHING LIMITED

Cover Illustration: Courtney Llloyd Robinson
Cover Design: Sanya Dockery
Book Design, Layout & Typesetting: Sanya Dockery

Published by LMH Publishing Limited
Suite 10-11, Sagicor Industrial Park
7 Norman Road
Kingston C.S.O., Jamaica
Tel.: (876) 938-0005;
Fax: (876) 759-8752
Email: lmhbookpublishing@cwjamaica.com
Website: www.lmhpublishing.com and www.lmhdigital.com

Printed in the U.S.A.   ISBN: 978-976-8245-43-4

NATIONAL LIBRARY OF JAMAICA CATALOGUING-IN-PUBLICATION DATA

Sylvester, Ditta
    Shameful shadows/ Ditta Sylvester

    p. ; cm .

ISBN 978-976-8245-43-4 (pbk)

1. Jamaican fiction
I. Title

813   dc 23

Contents

Acknowledgements

This book would not be complete, had I not acknowledged the contribution of those who have helped and supported me most.

My sincere thanks to my mother and to the memory of my father. Thanks to them both for teaching me the truth. Many thanks also to the others in my family for their kindness and understanding through the years, without which I would never have survived.

Special thanks to the faithful friends, like Joan and Lynda, who have 'stuck with me in my trials'. Also to Colin Reid, who gave me my first computer.

My biggest 'thank you', of course, goes to my God, for His providing me with those mentioned above, as well as for his generously supplying me with 'the power beyond what is normal'.

Ditta

CHAPTER ONE

Home Trouble

The work day had ended. Earl Masters cleaned himself up, got on his motorbike and headed home. Construction work was hard but rewarding. Nothing could beat the thrill of making something to rise from a hole in the ground and to tower into a strong, majestic building that could defy rain, wind, or whatever the elements chose to throw at it, and still stand tall – a silent monument to good craftsmanship.

He smiled. Today was Wednesday and Daisy would have finished cooking by now. A working man needed his yam and big dumplings, crowned with beautiful stew peas and nice chunks of pig's tail. Life with Daisy was good. They had been together for years now and he didn't regret a day of it. Pity he couldn't make her understand that when a man loved a woman as much as he loved her, there was really no need for them to get consent from any parson to live their lives as a happy couple, committed only to each other.

Except for that little fling some time ago, he had never been unfaithful to her, though he had often been tempted. He appreciated what he had and he knew he had to protect it. Earl respected his woman and he didn't want to lose her. He was sure that she was also true to him, but this business of marriage was beginning to get to him now.

Daisy had first begun to talk of marriage some years ago, when some church people had come into Elfin with their crusade. Earl saw himself as a God-fearing man but he hated the 'joyful noise' that those people insisted on making all the time. He didn't consider it joyful at all, especially after a hard day's work when he so dearly needed some shut-eye. Their God must have a hearing problem or something.

As he pulled into the yard, his young son came out to meet him.

"Hi, Daddy!" Peter greeted him.

"Hi, Pete," Earl replied. "Where is you madda an' sista?"

"Dem jus' leave out," the boy told him. "Pastor Abrams havin' a special service tonight."

Earl groaned within himself.

"Dinna cook?"

"Yes. It on di table. Mommy leave me to watch it for you."

"Oh. So dat is why she didn't carry you too." They shared a conspiratorial grin as Earl said, "You get weh tonight, boy!"

They both knew Daisy considered them both severely lacking in godliness.

Earl had a bath, then his dinner and sat down to watch a show with his son. The two were fast asleep when Winsome and her mother came in. As they shook them awake, Daisy asked, "Is di two a you a watch TV, or is TV watching you? An' wid di door wide open too!"

"Stop shake mi, Winsome!" Peter protested. "Me wake up now, man!"

Earl rubbed his eyes and said sleepily, "Is break di mike breakdown up a tent, tonight? I didn't hear one t'ing."

"Is a new preacher come tonight, Daddy," Winsome informed him. "Him nice bad! An' it look like him like mommy, too. Him follow us right to di gate."

"How you know is not you him like?" Daisy asked Winsome.

"Him betta not…" Earl said under his breath.

"Tell preacha not to like mommy," Peter said. "She don't like him. Is daddy she like."

"Is where you hear dat?" Daisy asked her son.

"You don't like me again, Mommy?" Earl asked in his baby voice.

The children giggled and Daisy ordered them to go to bed.

When they were alone, Earl asked Daisy about the new preacher but all she said was that he seemed to be a thoughtful man, whose preaching style was different from that of Pastor Adams.

"You like him?" Earl asked as they got into bed.

"I love all God's children," Daisy answered.

"But dat mus' mean say you don't love me, since you always say I am a child of Satan."

"Shut you mout' an' go sleep!" Daisy said, turning her back to him.

A few minutes later, she drew the covers over her head as he began to snore. She did not fall asleep for some time. The attention the new preacher gave her tonight had made her feel special. It wasn't that Earl did not pay attention to her. Quite the contrary. He was a good father who provided well for his family. But it seemed as though he was never going to get over his fear of marriage.

She had heard the story over and over. His mother and father had lived together for many years before getting married. Earl had never heard them quarrel before the wedding. It was his father who had been pushing the idea. His mother had married young and was divorced not long after. She had vowed never to remarry.

Not long after she was finally pressured into it by Earl's father, the couple began to have serious problems. His mother became a nag and his father – whom he had always known as a quiet, easy-going man – began to get jealous of every man who even looked at his wife.

He began to abuse her verbally and the first time he decided to beat her, Earl – their oldest – took him on. It wasn't many days later that he and his mother left the home he had always known, to live with an old aunt. His mother then found another man, who became the father of his half-sister. He had hated his mother's new boyfriend. As to his little sister, he didn't even like to talk about her. Nobody could convince Earl that his parents' marriage was not the cause of his family's breakup.

But she needed to get married, Daisy was thinking. It was long overdue and she was beginning to feel incomplete and somehow less than a woman. That was probably why, when the new preacher seemed to single her out for conversation and so much attention earlier that night, she had been so flattered.

She and Winsome had been looking forward to the special service and they arrived early.

Dennis Barton, the young preacher, had come over the moment he saw them come in.

"Good evening, ladies," he greeted them.

When they answered, he asked, "You looking for a seat?"

"Yes, Sir," Winsome told him.

"Sir!" Dennis exclaimed. "Am I your teacher, young lady?"

Winsome looked confused and couldn't find what to say.

Dennis laughed and told her, "Don't look so unhappy! I was just messing with you. People seldom call me 'sir' and I don't much like it when they do."

Then he placed himself between them both, extended his arms and asked them to hold on to him as he escorted them to a seat. Mother and daughter giggled self-consciously, as they placed their arms into his.

As he led them to be seated, Dennis said, "Look how close we are and I don't even know your name. I am Dennis."

"My name is Daisy. Dat is my daughter, Winsome."

"Happy to meet you both, Daisy and Winsome," Dennis replied. "Do you live in Elfin?"

"Yes," Winsome told him. "We live a few chains down dis road. Our house is di big white one at the corner."

"That's nice," Dennis said. "Do you go to school, Winsome?"

"Yes, Sir." But when she saw his disapproving look, Winsome corrected herself. "I mean yes, Dennis. I am going to high school."

"Good. And what do you do, Miss Daisy?"

"I jus' look after everyt'ing at home," she told him.

"Your husband is a lucky man," Dennis remarked.

Daisy said nothing. Then Dennis guided them to seats near to the podium and left. The two smiled quizzically at each other as he walked away.

Dennis was an excellent preacher. He had a voice which was booming and sensuous at the same time. He seemed to have little need for the microphone, as he moved up and down the podium, shouting down his message of the love of Jesus and the need for redemption. The crowd listened in silence as he told the story of how he had found God in prison.

He had been incarcerated some years ago for a terrible crime, he told his audience. He experienced no qualms of conscience for what he had done and was just languishing in prison, waiting for his opportunity to get out and do something even worse. He hated everybody, he told them, including himself. Then a priest had come to administer the last rites to a prisoner who was to be executed. That priest had taken the opportunity to speak to the other convicts, and that was when he had seen the light.

As he stomped and pranced all over the podium in the storm of his religious fervor, the glazed eyes of the audience followed him as though glued to the billowy folds of his long, black robe. Their faces shone, mesmerized, as they hung on to his every word. Lips trembled and tears flowed freely, as the preacher moved and spoke in the power of the spirit. Even the pins of the tent seemed to be caught up in the fire of holiness, as they rocked with the crowd.

Voices raised to echo, "Praise Him!"

When he yelled, "Can I get an amen?"

The crowd responded as one, "Aaaamen!"

But the preacher was not satisfied. He wanted more. More noise. Greater awe. Bigger and stronger excitement. More!

"Where is the amen for the Lord?" he yelled. "Can you say amen, my children? Can you say amen? Shout it! Scream it! Yell it! Say amen for Jesus!"

This time, the amen was loud enough to shake even the foundations of the ground on which they stood.

It was at this point that the ushers with the collection plates came around, and the yield in material gain that night was great. People gave without a thought of tomorrow's hungry belly, or fear of financial embarrassment. The service ended when Dennis led the crowd in an awesome, nerve-shaking rendition of the hymn *Glory*.

Winsome placed her hand in her mother's and the two were about to leave when Dennis called out to them, "Ladies, not so fast!"

The two stopped and waited as the preacher's long legs covered the distance between them.

"Leaving already?" Dennis asked, as he caught up with them.

"Yes," Daisy replied. "Is dark night now an' is only we two goin' our way."

"So let me walk with you," Dennis suggested.

"Oh…" Daisy hesitated. "We t'ank you, Preacha, but we can manage. Me an' Winsome always come to crusade up here an' we get home a'right. Is not so far."

"What kind of man would I be if I preached the love of God and didn't live it?" Dennis asked. "It is my duty to protect you."

There was no dissuading him so the three walked off into the night.

"Did you like the sermon?" Dennis asked, after a few steps.

"Oh, my!" Daisy responded. "Wonderful preaching, man, wonderful!"

"You goin' to be preaching tomorrow?" Winsome asked.

"Yes, and thanks a lot."

"Is what happen to Pastor Abrams?" Daisy asked. "I didn't see him tonight."

"Pastor Abrams is no longer a young man," Dennis replied. "I am here to help him. But enough about religion. Tell me about yourselves."

"I am in third form at school," Winsome said.

"And you?" Dennis said to Daisy.

She was beginning to feel a bit uncomfortable. The attention was nice, but why was this man showing so much interest in her and her daughter? She did not see what he had to gain from this so maybe, she figured, he was just naturally friendly.

8

"I am a housewife, as I tell you a'ready," she said.

"And the husband?" Dennis asked.

Daisy hesitated.

"My daddy is her fiancé," Winsome volunteered. "We are a happy family an' they soon get married."

"Great! I hope you'll remember to invite me," Dennis said, as Daisy breathed a sigh of relief.

The talk went back and forth between Dennis' sermon, the people of Elfin and the effect it might have on them. The preacher bade them good-night when he got to their gate, and the two thanked him and went in.

Dennis walked quickly back to the tent. The night air was cool and fresh. It reminded him of the many rural towns where his father had moved around and preached. That story of his life, which he had told the crowd an hour ago, had not been altogether true. He had embellished it for effect and felt no qualms about doing that. "The end justifies the means", his father had often remarked, after telling the audience a made-up story to "draw them to Christ".

His father had been a hard man. A stickler to the letter of the law, but totally without affection. Dennis had often wondered how different his life may have been, had he a mother, siblings and a generally normal family life. But his mother had died when he was born and his father had not remarried.

He strongly believed that it was this lack of love in his life that had driven him into the arms of Vinell Sarah Templeton. John Barton had chosen to pitch his tent in this very town, several years ago. It was summertime and he was out of school and with his father. John had determined, without much conferring with Dennis, that his son would be a preacher like himself. He had him enrolled him in a theological college, as soon as he had graduated from high school.

Dennis had met Shirley – as she had called herself – on the second night of the crusade in Elfin. He had never before seen a girl so beautiful.

She was not dressed conservatively like the other girls and he wondered if she really had intended to be there. Her full breasts strained at the bosom of her blouse, like wild horses on a starting block. Her skirt, which was much too short, exposed legs that to him – looked too nice to be used for something as ordinary as walking. He couldn't take his eyes off her and she knew it and was enjoying the effect she was having on him.

When their eyes met she smiled mischievously, sticking out her tongue at him. He stood transfixed, gazing at the young girl who was to cause him so much pain. That night, after the service was over and he was helping his father to get things together and out of the way, he saw her leaning against a tree in the near darkness. He knew she was waiting for him. Hurriedly, he finished up and told his father he needed to go for a short walk. That night, Dennis Barton lost his virginity to a girl who had not yet reached the age of consent.

He had been preparing to return to theological college after the holidays, when the police took him in custody for having committed statutory rape. As they took him away, his father loudly proclaimed that if Dennis were to be found guilty, he would no longer be his son. He was found guilty and sent to prison. True to his word, his father never came to see him, even once. It was when the older Mr. Barton passed away last year that Preacher Abrams, who had often travelled with them, had come to see him.

Mr. Abrams told Dennis that his father had had a change of heart, when he knew he was about to die. He had asked him to look up his son and to do what he could for him. That was when Abrams told him that if he could get out of prison early, he would take him on as a helper in his ministry.

Though he believed in God, Dennis had never been particularly attracted to the idea of preaching for a living. What was more, his father had been too much of an unpalatable mixture of piety and vengeance, for him to think much of his religion. In his heart, Dennis never thought of God as being loud, hard, excitable or judgmental. But he saw no other way out, so he buckled down to the business of reducing his sentence by doing everything right.

Frank Abrams kept his word. When Dennis was released a few months ago, he started planning this crusade with his new assistant as the main speaker. He had known him since he was born and he knew Dennis had inherited the gift of speaking and wooing a crowd from his father.

When he had visited Dennis in prison, he had given the young man the impression that he wanted to help him. But Frank also wanted to help himself. Since the demise of the older Mr. Barton, his crusades had been less than inspiring. The truth was, they were downright lackluster. He was losing more money than he gained when he went on the road to preach these days. He wasn't getting any younger and the day would soon come when he could no longer work. Frank needed a nest egg. So entered Dennis Barton.

When he got back to the tent, Preacher Abrams was counting the night's collection.

"We didn't do badly tonight, right?" Dennis asked.

"Not bad," the older man agreed.

"How much in all?" Dennis asked.

"Mmm…" Frank Abrams was reluctant to admit the figure. "Just wait 'til we finish weekend, man. You know you will get your fair share. Don't you trust me?"

"Of course!"

Daisy and both her children were present the following night. The crowd was even bigger. Dennis was in his element and the money kept pouring in. Then came the altar call. Even Peter was impressed as many came forward weeping, laying bare their sins, and confessing their desire to be cleansed by baptism.

Earl was home when the three got in. Peter excitedly told his father about what happened at the revival meeting. Then he asked, "Daddy, who is a fornicator?"

"What!" Earl was shocked.

Daisy cleared her throat and Winsome looked away.

"Why you askin' dat?" Earl said.

"Because preacha say tonight dat fornicators will not

inherit di kingdom and all fornicators must get baptized, to wash away dem sin," Peter explained.

"Well..." Earl hesitated.

When he said nothing more, Peter asked, "You don't know, Daddy?"

"No," his father told him, getting up. "Ask you mom 'bout dat."

"But is mommy tell me to ask you," Peter protested.

Earl flashed Daisy an angry look.

"Dat word is a church word," he told the boy. "I don't go to church an' if dat church lady can't help you, I don't see how I can."

With that, he walked away. It was Winsome who found the word in the dictionary and showed it to her brother.

Later that evening, as they got ready for bed, Daisy said to Earl, "You don't shame?"

"Shame? 'Bout what?" Earl asked.

"You don't shame to have to tell you son say you is a fornicator?"

"Don't worry come wid dat now," Earl said tiredly.

"How you mean? Is time we get married, Earl. Full time. It overdue now and dis situation is making me feel shame o' meself. I don't deserve dis. No sir!"

"Daisy, you know I work all day today. Give me little peace, man. Tomorrow we talk bout dat."

"Tomorrow," Daisy echoed him. "Tomorrow! Look how much tomorrow gone since mi an' you living in sin! How much more goin' to pass before you married to mi?"

"Dem children goin' to hear you, you know," Earl cautioned.

"I don't care if dem hear! I fed up wid dis situation now!"

"You know what?" Earl said, picking up his pillow. "I goin' sleep wid Pete tonight. You alone can go on wid you quarrelin'."

"You coulda sleep wid Peter for di rest of you life for all I care!" Daisy shouted at his back.

Earl did not get much sleep that night. Peter was not accustomed to having a bedmate and the boy kept tossing from one side of the bed to the other. As he lay awake, he told himself that maybe it wouldn't be such a bad idea for him to decide to marry Daisy. She fully deserved it. What was more, 'living in sin' seemed to be really getting to her nowadays. Never before had she quarrelled so loudly with him.

Life without marriage was becoming as stressful as he feared that life as a married man would be. It couldn't get much worse, so he might as well take the plunge.

CHAPTER TWO

Confrontation

ennis decided to walk about the town the following day. Everybody greeted him excitedly. It felt good and he responded as he thought he was expected to. If this continued, he would shortly become a celebrity, he told himself wryly. The truth was that he was much more interested in finding Shirley and his daughter, than he was in being a famous preacher. It had been a long time ago and all his enquiries had been fruitless, though he was still hopeful. A man needed people he could call his own.

He had just left the town square when he came face to face with Daisy.

"Hi, Miss Daisy!"

"Hi, Dennis! How you?"

"Fine. Where you heading to now?"

"Shop," Daisy answered. "I need some seasoning."

"Big cooking tonight?" Dennis asked.

"No. Jus' di usual."

"Oh."

"You look kinda lonely," Daisy said. "Why you don't come eat wid us dis evening?"

"Me? You sure that's okay, Miss Daisy?"

"Of course!" she assured him.

"Okay. What time?"

"About six o'clock."

"Thanks," Dennis said happily. "See you later."

He arrived early at the Masters' house. His excuse was that he had to preach that night, so he needed to eat early. The truth was, he was lonely. Daisy had not been expecting him so soon. She had only just turned off the stove and the children, who had gone to the library that evening, had not yet returned home. She decided to feed Dennis before the others.

She sat at the table and watched him as he ate.

"It a'right?" she asked.

"It's fine, thank you!" Dennis told her. "I could never get tired of rice and chicken."

"Glad you like it. You don't mind eatin' alone?"

"Always have," Dennis replied. "And I'm not really alone. You are here. You looking a little sad today, though. Everything alright?"

Daisy was hesitant to tell this stranger her personal problems.

"Well, everyt'ing not goin' to be perfectly a'right every-day," she said. "How 'bout you? A nice young man like you should get a wife, married an' settle down."

"That will come, Miss Daisy," Dennis said.

"Don't put it off too long."

The minutes passed. The silence between them was pleasant and comfortable like they had known each other for years. Then he asked her, "Long time you living here?"

"Yes. I born an' grow in dis very town," Daisy told him.

"Really? You know anybody living here name Shirley?"

"Shirley? No. What is her last name?"

"Templeton," Dennis said. "Shirley Templeton."

"No. I don't know anybody from here by dat name. But dat sound like a movie star name." Daisy laughed. "You sure dat girl tell you her right name?"

Dennis said nothing. He was almost sure the girl had another name. He knew he had heard it somewhere, but just couldn't remember what it was. Then she asked him to describe the girl. When he did, something stirred in her eyes.

"You know her?" Dennis asked hopefully.

But Daisy shook her head.

"Is a girlfrien'?" she asked.

"Maybe."

"How you mean maybe? Dat sound like a yes to me. You try find her an' married to her, before you reach my stage. A woman need a stable marriage to be really happy."

He knew she was talking about herself.

"I know it is not my business but your fiancé is a fool to put off marrying you! But it will happen for you, Miss Daisy. Don't worry."

Daisy couldn't hide the feeling of self-pity which suddenly overwhelmed her. She put her head on the table and wept quietly. Dennis' first impulse was to reach out and try to comfort her but something told him this was not the appropriate thing to do. He got up and stood uncertainly behind her.

"I can see he is a good provider and I know you love him," Dennis sympathized. "That is why you stay. I am sure he will do the right thing soon."

It was about that same point in time Earl came walking into his yard. He had had a terrible day. He had woken up late and arrived late at work. He hadn't even bothered to stop to eat, though he felt sure that Daisy would have made him breakfast. He had to do right by that woman. She was so good to him and his children. He would be buying her a ring very, very soon.

It may have been his empty stomach or lack of sleep that caused him not to check that the ladder and everything else was safely in place before sending two men to work on the roof. The younger man had managed to save himself but the older had fallen and was now in the hospital. He had shut down work for the day and sent the men home early. He was about a mile from his own home when he ran out of gas. He parked the bike at a friend's house and walked the rest of the way home.

As he approached the house, he heard a voice he did not know. Earl crept stealthily closer to a window and was just in time to hear Dennis say:

"You are a good woman and love brings sweet rewards. No matter how long we may have to wait."

Earl did not wait for another word. He ran up the steps, noisily pushed the front door open and shouted, "Is what goin' on here? Is who you, Mister?"

"Earl!" Daisy exclaimed, jumping up from the table.

"Is who dis telling you 'bout love an' sweet rewards, Daisy?"

"Dis is Dennis, di preacha, an' is not dat him did mean!"

"I don't know what him mean but I know what I hear," Earl said, as he shortened the distance between him and Dennis. "What di hell you doing inna my house, talkin' to my woman 'bout love!" he yelled.

"Listen to me, Earl," Daisy pleaded, placing herself between the two men. "Dis is not what you believe it is."

"Come way inside a man house come a talk 'bout love!" Earl continued heedlessly. "Jus' come out a my way mek I get fi bus' dis preacha boy arse, you hear mi, Daisy?"

Dennis was more than a little alarmed but he stood his ground.

"Miss Daisy is a lady I respect," he told Earl. "All I was saying to her is that if you love her, you will marry her eventually."

This little speech did not help matters much. Earl turned his anger on Daisy now. "So is dis little pissin' tail boy you have to invite inna we house fi tell we business, Daisy? You let mi down, man. Jus' get him outa here right now, before I lick him down!"

Then he walked away, muttering angrily to himself. Dennis made his exit as fast as he could. When Daisy found him, Earl was still mumbling to himself.

"Dat is why I jus' don't like dis married business, you know," he was saying. "Jus' as I decide say we goin' finally do somet'ing, look what happen!"

"Is what you decide seh now, an' is what you see happen?" Daisy asked him.

"Nutten," Earl answered belligerently. "You know say is only you I want, so I don't know what you worrying yourself 'bout. I totally confuse now. I even more 'fraid fi married, now. I don't know what to do!"

"Well, I know," Daisy said. "I goin' give you a little time by youself. I goin' up to Ingram to spen' little time."

Earl gazed at her in silence.

"Is leave you leavin' mi, Daisy?" he asked.

"No. I just want to go spend little time wid Miss Eva an' Pauline."

"So who goin' look after me an' dem children?"

"I not stayin' long. You and dem will manage till I get back. Suppose mi did dead?"

Earl could find no appropriate answer to that question. Still, he begged her not to go. But Daisy was adamant.

And he blamed the whole situation on the institution of marriage.

When Dennis got back to the tent site that night he told Abrams what happened at Daisy's house.

"That was a close one," the older man said. "Women can get a man into serious trouble, Dennis."

"But all I went there for was a meal," Dennis replied. "Of course I like Daisy and her family. But we are all just good friends."

"So what about the girl?" Abrams asked with an unholy gleam in his eyes.

"You mean, Winsome?"

"Yes. That's a buxom one!"

Dennis looked at him in surprise.

"I didn't think you would notice that," he said.

"I am a man, my boy. Just like any other man."

"You know, I've known you all my life but I don't know very much about you," Dennis said. "Have you ever been in love?"

Abrams didn't answer immediately. He was remembering how much he had been in love with Dennis' mother. She had been a pretty, young thing when they had met at bible school; young, vivacious and different. Not the type of girl one would expect to choose the ministry as a career. He had been head over heels in love and they had planned on getting married. Until Dennis' father came along. Margaret had discarded him like a torn glove and married his friend and colleague.

He had learned to live with the pain but he had never quite forgotten that loss. People talked about forgiving and forgetting but it wasn't that easy. He had consoled himself with the thought that at least he would have command of the money which Dennis' mother, father and he made from their evangelizing activities.

He had been good at it too. They had never quite figured out that he had, for years, been siphoning off much more than his fair share of the profits. This didn't make him feel guilty. He was simply paying them back for the pain they had caused him, he figured. It was justice.

When Margaret died in childbirth, John Barton had taken it hard. He knew that was why he was so hard on Dennis. He had blamed the boy for his loss. Frank had continued to take care of the planning and the financial side of things, always making sure his own nest was comfortably feathered.

On one of their crusades, he had seen a young woman whom he had deeply desired from the first time he saw her. She was a child, in fact. A luscious, beautiful little thing, who reminded him of so much of his lost love. She could easily have been his daughter; his and Margaret's. By that time, he had enough money to make any woman comfortable but he was afraid to approach her. He was sure she would have laughed at an old man like himself.

He would have to put her out of his mind, he told himself. He would find himself a woman closer to his own age, among the many who attended their crusades. There were several in attendance even that night, whom he could have had just for the asking.

But Frank liked them young. The younger, the better. So when he saw the girl giving Dennis the eye, something began to boil inside him. Were his feelings again to be trampled upon by another Barton? He could barely contain himself. Frank felt sure that if he were a younger man, he would have murdered Dennis that night. He watched as the girl waited for the boy. He heard when he told his father that he was going for a walk, and he followed him.

Even now he could hear, in his mind, the sounds of their lovemaking in the bushes. He had watched and waited in the darkness. He thought he would have gone mad for sure. As he watched and listened, a fire which demanded to be quenched, was ignited in his loins. But he managed to keep quiet till they were through.

He had followed them in the shadows as Dennis had attempted to walk the girl home. Before they reached her house, however, she convinced him to turn back. Obviously, she did not want him to know where she lived. But Frank had continued to follow her. He watched her go in. Then he moved stealthily into the yard and found a tree against which to lean himself. From there, in the near-darkness, he kept watching the girl through her window.

Minutes passed. He was not sure what to do but he knew he had to do something. He could not return to face two generations of Bartons doing him out of a woman. Then he bent over, took up some of the gravel that lay at his feet and tentatively threw one at the window. She stopped and listened for a moment before returning to what she had been doing. Then he threw another.

She came to the window then and whispered, "Dennis?"

"Yes!" he whispered back, not moving. He couldn't let her see him. "I have something for you."

"What?" she asked quietly.

"Come and you will see."

"So it can't wait till tomorrow?"

"No. Come now."

"But..."

"I have to leave early tomorrow morning."

Then he waited for her in the darkness.

"Dennis?" she said, coming closer.

"Over here," he whispered.

"Is who show you mi house?" she enquired, coming closer.

When she was close enough, he grabbed her and put his hand over her mouth.

"I am not Dennis," he told her. "I don't want to harm you but you must do as I say. All you have to do is give me what you gave Dennis, a few minutes ago."

The girl shook her head vigorously in protest and he continued, "You want me to call out your mother now and tell her what you an' Dennis just do in the bush? I have money to give you."

He let go of her, when he felt sure that she was ready to obey.

"Well, have you ever been in love?" Dennis asked again.

Abrams cleared his throat, pulling himself away from his memories.

"Yes, I've been in love," he said vacantly. "Twice; with the same woman."

"I don't understand," Dennis confessed.

"Neither do I," the older man said.

CHAPTER THREE
An Affair to Forget

Vinell knew for sure that she was pregnant, after she had missed her second period. She had by now been used to getting into trouble but this had been the most serious so far. She had surely outdone herself this time. But what else was there to do? She had nobody who really cared about her. Well, not really nobody; but that particular somebody was just too overbearing sometimes.

She was sure that her brother cared and she knew he was trying to fill in for her missing father, but she was certainly not about to put up with his pushing her around. She wasn't even sure that her real father really existed. She had seen him a few times when she was little, but he had his own family and a wife who was not her mother. On the rare occasions he visited her mother and her, he was always in a hurry to leave and she always got the feeling that he felt like he was in the wrong place.

Her mother was also frequently missing. Vinell knew she had been married but couldn't remember ever seeing her mother's husband. Neither of those men had any interest in either one of them. So what did that make her? An outcast, she concluded. So as soon as she realized she was becoming a woman, with the ability to seduce men, she decided that she would no longer be an outcast. She would have any man she wanted.

She had seen Dennis long before he saw her and she wanted him. She was sure she would be able to seduce him – preacher's son or not. Hell, she could seduce any man she had a mind to. He had a good-looking face, nice soft eyes and a brownish complexion. Dennis was friendly, fiery and exciting - definitely her type. She had told him that her name was Shirley. She hated the name Sarah. She had seen Shirley Temple in an old movie one time, and decided that though that girl must have been a star of long ago, 'Shirley Templeton' sounded much classier than 'Vinell Templeton'.

It had been fun being with him too. Pity she couldn't say the same about the creepy old man who came later. He was disgusting; threatening her about telling her mother. Old fool! Like Eva cared a hoot about her or what she was up to. But if Earl had found out about her night time carryings-on, there would have been hell to pay. He would prevent her from ever going out on her own again, she felt sure. Worse still, her brother might have decided to send her back home to Ingram. So she had given in.

That was the first time she had ever felt dirty after having sex. It had been very unpleasant and she told herself that was what rape must feel like. She spent a long time washing herself of him, after he had left.

She had taken the man's money but was surprised to find that she didn't really want it. Having it made her feel ashamed and really bad about herself. She thought of giving it to her little niece, but she felt sure that Daisy or Earl would find out and ask where she had gotten it. On the last night of the crusade, making sure Dennis did not see her, she had put Pastor Abram's money back into his collection plate.

The only thing that made being pregnant bearable, was that she still thought fondly of her baby's father. Nice, cute Dennis! She had known all about contraceptives but had been too excited about her new conquest to remember anything like that. She was only a few weeks shy of her sixteenth birthday when she gave birth.

The delivery was the most horrible thing she had ever experienced, and she vowed never to let that happen to her again. She wasn't planning on being any doting mother but was curious to see what the child looked like. At least she could dress it up like a nice, pretty little dolly and show it off when she had a mind to.

Vinell stood by the bed and gazed with disapproval at her newborn. She was shocked and felt terribly cheated. All the suffering she had endured for nine long months was for this - this squalling, messy little thing! As soon as she was sure that she could walk without falling, she packed her bag and left the hospital, not to be seen by her relatives for a very long time.

It was her mother, Eva, who took the baby and brought her home. She named her Pauline.

Eva Masters was combing her granddaughter's hair. She was trying to be gentle but every now and again, the child would gasp with pain.

"Hush, baby!" Eva said. "I soon finish."

Pauline wiped her eyes and asked, "Why some people have bad hair, Grandma?"

"Bad hair? What you talking about Pauline? Bad hair! Nobody have anyt'ing name bad hair."

"But is so dem children at school call it."

"So all dem children have straight hair?"

"No."

"Listen to me, girl," Eva said. "God give some people straight hair, some kinky hair and some curly. Just like how we have so many different color flowers, is so we have many different kind and color of hair an' skin. Suppose we did have only white flowers? You believe dis world would look so pretty?"

Pauline smiled.

"How you so wise, Grandma?"

"I wasn't always wise, baby," Eva said. "But you live and you learn."

"Will I have to be old like you before I get wise?" the child asked with a grin.

"If you wise, you will keep you head an' you mouth quiet an' don't ask me any more feisty question!" Eva told her granddaughter.

This one was her chance for redemption from the guilt she felt over the poor example she had set for her own children, Eva told herself. Her adulterous relationship with Keith

28

Templeton had been her downfall. It had broken up her life and her marriage. She should have had the strength to ignore her feelings for that city slicker, in the interest of her family.

She had not really been in love when she had hooked up with Earl's father. He had given her a sense of security at a time when she was on the rebound from a failed teenage marriage. She had grown to respect the man and was willing to spend the rest of her life with him, though she never really loved him as much as a woman should love her man. And that was why she had been reluctant to marry him.

Then she had met Vinell's father and fallen in love with him. It was when she found out that he was already married, that she had finally agreed to marry Herbert Masters.

It had felt wrong before it even happened. She knew she was marrying Herbert for all the wrong reasons but she felt that somehow her status as a married woman would keep her faithful to her husband, and keep the family together. It hadn't worked. She kept on meeting Keith as often as she could, though she knew that Herbert was sure to find out sometime. When he did, he became violent and she knew it was the end for her and him. She had just discovered that she was pregnant with Vinell when they parted.

The young Earl had been her hero. The two younger children had stayed behind with their father and she had altogether lost touch with them. Aunt Mary, who then lived alone, had been happy to have them. Herbert had continued to maintain them financially but when Vinell was little more than a toddler, she decided to tell him the truth. That he was not her baby's father.

He had taken it badly. Though he knew she had been unfaithful, Herbert could not get past the idea of her carrying another man's child. Their final parting had been loud and painful. And still Earl had continued to take her side.

They had been in a terrible fix when Herbert had cut them off, with hardly enough to eat. Most of the time, they had to be content with eating flour and margarine. After Earl had complained one evening that the dumplings were "smaller dan a big button", Eva decided to contact Keith. She threatened that she would tell his wife about Vinell, if he continued to refuse to give financial support to his daughter.

She got some money from him then, but Keith harbored resentment over her having threatened him. Herbert had filed for divorce and she no longer had a relationship with her new daughter's father, so Eva was at a loose end.

Earl was the only man in her life now. As soon as he could find work, he began providing for his little sister and mother. That, with the money she received from Vinell's father, made life fairly good for them. The only thing Eva had to complain about was her loneliness.

She met Stanley Jones shortly after Vinell had turned seven. He was a builder to whom Earl had been apprenticed. It was a Friday evening and he had come to find out why Earl – who was in bed with the flu – had not turned up for work. He had told her how good a worker Earl was and how quickly he was learning the trade. His hand had touched and lingered on hers, as he gave her Earl's pay for the week. Their eyes met and he gave her a wink. Before he left, he promised to scold Earl for not telling him what a pretty mother he had.

They went to a show the following weekend. They were heading back home in his car when she asked him why he was still single.

"Just lookin' for my soul mate," Stanley answered her. "An' maybe I just find her too," he added, smiling at her.

Eva returned his smile but turned her face away. Yes, she was lonely but her past experiences had taught her to be cautious where men were concerned.

"What about you children?" she enquired.

Stanley hesitated a little before he said, "I have a boy an' a girl. Dem living abroad with dem mother."

"So you all keep in touch?" she asked next.

"I talk to mi children all di time. Sometime I call an' sometime dem call me. But mi and dem mom mash up long time."

"You right to keep in touch wid you children," Eva said. "Dem permanent in America?"

"No. Is not too long since dem gone up, but dem mother live a 'Merica long time. She supposed to be helpin' dem to work on dem papers."

Eva wanted to ask him if he had a visa or was planning on joining them but she didn't want to appear to be too nosey. When they got to her house, he tried to kiss her but she pushed him away playfully and told him "next time".

The next time came two weeks later. They had gone to watch a particularly sad and enthralling love story. Eva was trying hard not to let him see her tears. She didn't want him to consider her soft or foolish. Then, to her surprise, she saw that Stanley was crying too. And that was what won her over.

She was sure that he wasn't pretending. Except for her first husband, Jay, Eva had seldom ever seen a grown man cry. Once or twice at a funeral, maybe, but never at a movie. Only Jay – the dreamer – would react like this. Poor, funny, childlike Jay! Their marriage had been doomed before it had even begun. Happily, their union had produced no children.

But this man sitting beside her was no child. He was definitely for real. He could experience tender feelings without being afraid or embarrassed to show it. She had for so long wanted a man who could be strong, and yet not feel compelled to impress her with being macho all the time. She saw herself watching and enjoying many more features of life with Stanley Jones.

They slept together for the first time that night. Aunt Mary had passed away the year before, so Eva now had her own bedroom in the house. Earl was a bit embarrassed by the whole thing and avoided looking directly at his mother for days. He felt sure this would affect his relation-ship with his employer but it didn't. If anything, Stanley treated him even better than he used to.

He couldn't but accept the new situation as his boss began spending more and more time at the house. At least his mother seemed happier than she had been in quite some time and that was important to him. Things didn't feel exactly right but he decided to go quietly with the flow, since he could not do otherwise.

Stanley had just left one morning and Earl was also on his way out, when Vinell asked him, "Mum boyfrien' is our new daddy, Earl?"

"Not my daddy," Earl told her. "I jus' work for him."

"So is my daddy?" the little girl asked.

"No, Nelly. Don't you remember you own daddy? Him sen' a dolly for you last Christmas."

"Oh, yes," Vinell said. "But I did fling dat dolly inna river long time."

"What!" Earl said. "Why?"

"I didn't want no dolly. Is a daddy I did want."

Earl looked at the child with compassion in his eyes. Then he stooped down and hugged her close.

"Who is Nelly big, bad brother?" he asked her.

"You," Vinell said, smiling.

"Who will kill an' beat an' mash up anybody who try to trouble Nelly?"

"You."

"Who will always love and take care of baby button-nose, Nelly?"

"I am not no baby!" Vinell objected, trying to pull away. "An' I don't have any button nose!"

Earl held her fast.

"Ansa mi question!" he commanded.

"You," Vinell admitted.

"Right," Earl continued. "So why you worrying 'bout daddy, daddy every day?"

"Because you not mi daddy."

He felt defeated but he didn't show it. Instead, he said, "If you promise to be happy and to stop worryin', I promise to get you something nice Friday evening."

"What?"

"What you want?" Earl asked.

Vinell thought hard before she said, "Maybe you could buy me a dolly in place of di one I did fling weh."

"Good," Earl replied. He kissed her on the cheek and said, "Be a good girl today an' don't give mum any trouble."

"Yes, Daddy," the little girl answered.

Earl's heart ached as he turned to go. Poor, poor little Nell! She could be a handful but he loved her so much. He vowed never to allow a child of his to feel so abandoned and alone. Then his mind went to Daisy.

He had met her a few weeks ago, when Stanley had employed her to cook for the workmen that day. Her cooking was enough to make him desire her but Daisy was much more than a good cook. She looked nice and he admired her dignified attitude and quiet demeanor.

At the end of the work day, he had asked Stanley where she came from. He learned from his employer that Daisy was the niece of a friend of his who lived in Elfin. That same weekend, Earl bought himself some new clothes and shoes and set out to find Daisy Bishop.

Elfin was a small country town much like Ingram and only about five miles away.

It had a few small shops, a library and a post office. He had passed through there once or twice since his mother had come to live in Ingram. Maybe it was how the land lay that made it such a charming place.

The houses were fairly far apart and between them lay large, rolling fields of guinea grass. The people of Elfin owned more cattle than most other village or town people did.

Visitors to the town were always amazed at the way the cows moved about the place almost as freely as the children. This gave the place a quality so picturesque and surreal, it could well have emerged from the pages of a child's story book.

The cattle kept the grass cropped at an acceptable height and generally left their droppings in the fields, and out of sight. Newcomers, who used to be scared of cows, usually lost that phobia as they watched the children pet the animals as each passed the other. The moment a cow was found to be developing a temper or acting wild, its owner would promptly catch it and sell it to the butcher.

Earl smiled as he rode his bicycle past one such field, the Saturday evening he had gone in search of Daisy. This could be a nice place for me to build a house for her, he said to himself. He stopped when he came to the post office. Stanley had told him that his friend lived not too far from there. He was not too sure what to do next. He was waiting for somebody approachable to pass, to ask if that person knew her, when he saw Daisy herself walking down the street.

His heart jumped. What would he say to her? It was too late for him to hide since she had already seen him, so he leaned against his bicycle and tried to look as worldly and debonair as he could. Daisy walked up to where he was standing, gave him a quizzical look and walked right on past. Earl was disappointed that she hadn't recognized him but he wasn't about to give up.

"Hi, Miss!" he called.

She stopped and looked back.

"Yes?"

"You don't rememba me?"

"Rememba you from where?"Daisy enquired.

"I was on di work site wid Mr. Jones when you did come cook for we," he told her.

"Oh. I didn't know you live round here."

"Well..." Earl hesitated. "Is really up Ingram I live."

"So what you doing down here?"Daisy asked.

He could hide it no longer.

"Is...is you I come to look for," he said haltingly.

Daisy said nothing. She continued to walk but more slowly, and he rode beside her.

Earl wasn't much of a speaker and his style of expressing his interest was neither fluent nor original, but Daisy could detect that he was sincere and she agreed to go out with him some time soon. Before very long, their relationship blossomed into love and the two were spending as much time as they could together. Eventually, Earl brought his lady home to meet his mother and sister.

Daisy felt quite at ease with Eva when they met. But the moment Vinell laid eyes on the woman she considered to be a rival for her brother's affection, she hated her. Earl put his hand on her head as he introduced her to Daisy as his little sister, Nelly.

"Hi, Nelly," Daisy said with a smile.

Vinell said nothing. Daisy could see the resentment in the child's face and she was more than willing to leave things as they were. Earl was not.

"Say 'hi' to Auntie Daisy," Earl encouraged his sister.

"If she was my auntie, I would kill myself!" Vinell said rudely. "Why you couldn't find a pretty girl who could dress an' talk good, Earl?"

Earl was appalled and he scolded her firmly. Eva was shocked and embarrassed. She told her daughter to apologize but Vinell refused and was sent outside. Though Earl apologized profusely for his sister's behavior, the atmosphere was tense and uncomfortable for the rest of the evening. Daisy told herself that if she were ever to have a meaningful relationship with Earl, she would have to steer clear of this unpleasant child.

Vinell was pleased. At least she had stuck up for herself, she was thinking as she stormed out of the house. At least she had made them feel as badly as she did. It wasn't really the person of Daisy that was the problem. She looked alright. It was just that Daisy was the person who had come barging into their lives now, with the intention – she was convinced – of stealing her brother's attention away from her.

Earl was the only one in her life who truly cared about her feelings. Unlike her mother, he never regarded her or treated her like a 'little mistake'. Earl really loved her and as far as she knew, he was the only person who did. What would she do when he was gone?

Daisy got pregnant with her first child when Vinell was about ready to enter high school. By this time, Earl had moved into a small place which he had rented for his girlfriend. Except for Vinell's behavior, which seemed to get worse every day, things were going fairly well for Eva and her family. Stanley was a generous man and he made sure they never wanted for anything. He moved in shortly after Earl moved out.

Eva had been going through his pockets prior to doing the laundry one day, when she found a letter. Like most women would, she read it. It had been written by a woman, whose address was somewhere in New York. From its contents, she deduced that the writer was the mother of Stanley's two children. Eva nearly fainted when she read that the woman was reminding him of their plans to get married, so that he could migrate to America to be with the rest of his family.

That evening as he was having dinner, Eva asked, "You have a visa, Stan?"

"No. I can't worry wid dat visa foolishness. Too much trouble an' waste a time. You have one?"

"No," Eva told him.

"I not worryin' 'bout dat at all. I have a good life here. I get plenty work an'"– he paused to smile at her – "I have a good woman now. I don't interested in goin' a 'Merica."

Eva smiled but she said nothing. After a while she asked, "You keep in touch wid you children, mom?"

Stanley looked up.

"Look how long I tell you say me an' she mash up long time? I keep in touch wid mi children. Hyacinth love write but I don't answer her."

Hyacinth! That was the name that was signed at the bottom of the letter. Eva sat very still. She knew not what to say or do. Maybe she ought to trust this man. After all, it was Hyacinth who was trying to force herself on him. Maybe she should just try to ignore this nonsense and concentrate on living her life to the fullest with this wonderful man.

"You a'right?" Stanley asked, watching her.

"Yes," she said, getting up. "Excuse me a little."

She went into her room and locked the door. Eva took the letter from where she had hidden it and read it again. Hyacinth had signed as 'your darling forever'. Eva repeated the words and hissed her teeth. Why couldn't this woman accept the fact that Stanley was over and done with her? If only she could lay her hands on her! Then Hyacinth would discover, first-hand, just what she thought of her trying to take Stanley away!

The weeks went quietly by and Stanley was as supportive and loving as ever. He was patient with even the rebellious

Vinell, whose main objective seemed to be to get on everybody's nerves.

On the Wednesday before Christmas, he left early and told her that he would be back late, since he would be going into Kingston to buy building materials. When Earl came by later that day, she asked him if he knew of his employer's whereabouts and he repeated the same story that Stanley had told her.

But he did not return that night. The Thursday after, somebody brought her a message from him. A relative of his who lived in town was seriously ill and in the hospital. The rest of the family had asked him to stick around for moral support, so he would have to be away for a few days. Eva did not doubt this story for a minute and waited patiently for her lover to return.

Stanley came back the following week. He reported that his cousin was now much better and that everything should be fine from then on. When Eva asked about the new clothes he had brought back, he told her that his sister - who had a green card - had brought them for him from America some time ago. Since he had taken no clothes with him, they had come in very useful.

In the months that followed, the relationship between Stanley and Eva seemed to get even better than it formerly was, and any doubt which may have lingered at the back of her mind, had vanished. Hyacinth had been grasping at straws, she was convinced. Stanley had moved on. She, Eva, was now the only 'darling' in his life.

She felt sure that he would be popping the question any time now and just as sure, that her third marriage would be the one that would make her life complete.

CHAPTER FOUR
Pauline

Winsome Masters came into the world on a cool November night. By this time, Earl had secured the lease on a small plot of land and had started work on his house. Eva was very proud of her first granddaughter and son. She visited them often and got on well with Daisy. Though Earl was no longer apprenticed to Stanley, the two men remained friends.

Earl thought he would never finish building the house. He worked all week to support his family and worked on the house on weekends. Stanley gave him free labor as often as he could. Now and again, he would also send him a bag or two of cement, which he had managed to pilfer from whatever job he was working on at the time.

The holidays were approaching that year and Eva was busily fixing up the place one evening, when Stanley said to her, "I goin' to have to go out tomorrow."

"Out where?" Eva asked.

"To town. My sista just sen' few more t'ings for me for di holiday."

"Oh. You stayin' long?"

"No, man! Don't you know I can't stay away from you too long?"

Eva smiled contentedly.

She was sitting in the yard the day after Stanley had left, wondering why he hadn't called or sent a message. Maybe he had been detained by his relatives this time again. A twig broke in the bushes behind her and she spun around, startled. Vinell was standing there with the familiar impudent smirk on her face.

"You know you frighten me!" Eva said angrily. "Is what you up to now?"

"I not 'up to' anyt'ing, as you call it," Vinell answered.

"So what you want?"

Vinell leaned against the breadfruit tree.

"Why Stanley carry him suitcase if him plan to come back?" she asked her mother.

"You hear I tell you not to call him Stanley," Eva scolded. "Him is a big man to you. You have no manners at all!"

"Why him carry him suitcase?" Vinell repeated.

"To put what him going for, into!" Eva replied impatiently. "What dat have to do wid you? You wash out you clothes dem yet?"

"No."

"So is me you expect to wash for a big girl like you?" Eva asked.

"Might as well," Vinell said. "You not goin' to have much to wash for Stanley again."

"What! What you mean by dat now?"

"You didn't notice dat him carry most of him clothes wid him yesterday?" Vinell asked.

"Why you so lie, Vinell?"

"An' him shoes dem, too," Vinell continued.

Eva glared at her daughter in disbelief. Her mouth opened to contradict her but she said nothing. Instead, she got up hurriedly and ran into the house. Frantically, she looked through closets, drawers and under the bed she had shared with Stanley. And as the truth of her lover's betrayal dawned on her, Eva knew she would never ever trust another man.

She sat down heavily on the bed. She still couldn't believe it. Maybe there was a logical explanation. There had to be. Stanley would never do this to her. Not her Stan. Not the man she had loved and depended on for so long. But his passport and driver's license were missing too.

Then she became aware that Vinell was standing in the doorway, staring at her. She looked back at her daughter. There was the look of quiet, insolent derision on the girl's face again. Even now, when she was fully aware of the pitiful state she was in, the child was choosing to mock instead of trying to sympathize with, or console her. Suddenly, she lost it.

Eva knew she was being irrational for blaming the child for what had gone wrong in her life, but she couldn't help it. It was the birth of Vinell that had caused the failure of her second marriage. Vinell, who had caused her break-up with

Keith. Vinell, who kept disrespecting Stanley and calling him out of his name. Vinell, who now saw it fit to alert her to Stanley's leaving. Vinell. Vinell. Vinell. Everything, Vinell.

Without warning, logic took the wings of frustration and pain and flew – at least temporarily – out of Eva Masters' mind. She so wanted to erase – once and for all – this mistake of hers, which had suddenly assumed such diabolical proportions. She looked around the room. Her eyes fell upon a large, stinky boot Stanley had left behind. Eva lunged, picked it up and – in the same unbroken motion – flung it with all her might at her daughter.

It caught Vinell full in the face. The girl was stunned. This was the last thing she had expected. Then all the resentment she had harbored for so long, against this woman who claimed to be her mother, broke loose. What started out looking like corporal punishment at its most extreme, erupted into a cat fight between two women. They fought with equal venom but the element of youthful vigor, added much more fury to Vinell's blows.

It was the neighbors who came and pulled the girl off her mother. By the time Earl heard the news and got to Ingram, Eva had already been taken by a friend to the doctor. He was thankful the crowd had dispersed by the time he got there. He was ashamed and felt partly responsible that things had turned out this way, for his mother and sister.

That night, Earl gave his sister the flogging he thought she deserved and Vinell felt – for the first time in her life – that her brother hated her too.

Her granddaughter was her whole life now, Eva told herself as she finished combing Pauline's hair. She had never quite gotten over the pain of Stanley's abandonment, though Earl had come to her rescue financially and otherwise.

It was he who had told her, as gently as he could, how he had learned that her lover had gone into town on the week before Christmas, to meet and marry Hyacinth. She was the 'sister' with the green card of whom Stanley had spoken. His final departure had come, after her filing for his immigration to the United States had come through.

But that was then, Eva thought. Pauline was now her only and best significant other.

"Now who is my pretty little baby girl?" she asked, holding the child's face between her hands.

Pauline smiled.

"You really t'ink I pretty, Grandma?" she asked.

"I don't just t'ink you pretty. I know for sure dat you pretty. I almost sure dat I see it somewhere in my Bible dat Pauline Masters is a very, very pretty girl!"

"Dat is not true!" Pauline said, laughing. "Uncle Earl say I look like my mother. Is true, Grandma?"

Eva cleared her throat. She always avoided talking about Vinell to Pauline. It was too painful.

"Don't you say you want to wear you new dress today?" she asked, side-stepping the question.

"Yes!" Pauline said excitedly.

"Well, go bathe now an' stop questioning mi."

Pauline hurried away.

Eva watched the child with pride. She enjoyed going out with her. She was a bright, well-mannered little girl who always made her look good in public. So unlike her mother. Then her mind flashed back to the last time she had appeared in public with Vinell.

They had been in court. Even now she could see, in her mind's eye, the prisoner in the dock; a young, innocent-looking boy. He didn't even seem to fully understand what was happening to him. Either that or he was too dazed to believe it.

Vinell's state of pregnancy had just very recently been discovered at the time. She – Eva – had not even been the first to hear about it. At the time, she had still not fully recovered from Stanley's betrayal. Daisy had agreed with Earl, that the girl should spend some time with them and away from her mother. So Vinell went to live at her brother's house. Daisy, who was pregnant with her second child, was not particularly fond of the idea but she liked Eva and felt it her duty to help.

Surprisingly, Vinell fitted much better into her brother's home, than she had done in her own. Earl had moved into the new house as soon as one of the rooms was completed. Since then, he had done much more work on it, though it was still not yet fully made. It was a big house so she got her own room. She did chores around the house and was generally quiet and co-operative. She even seemed to like her little niece, Winsome.

It was only on the matter of her leaving the house to go out at nights that Vinell and her brother butted heads. She was coming into her womanhood, and she knew it and was proud of it. She found it a new and exciting pastime to show off her physical attributes when most of the young men had come off work and were out and about the town. Daisy was having a difficult pregnancy and couldn't help him much with that, so Earl told Vinell she could go out at night, but only if she kept a strict curfew.

She kept the curfew and Earl was pleased and rewarded her with some money to buy new clothes. What he did not know, was that after his sister politely said goodnight to the family, she would frequently climb back out through her window and down the custard apple tree, to meet with a male friend.

It was Daisy who first suspected that Vinell was pregnant, after she had heard her bringing up back her breakfast quite a few mornings. She decided to check whether she had been using the feminine products she had provided for her. She hadn't. When she spoke to her about the matter, Vinell replied that she had forgotten they were there and had bought some for herself. Daisy was not satisfied and advised Earl to take his sister to the doctor, since she seemed to be developing a bad stomach.

When he discovered that she was indeed carrying a baby, Daisy worried that Earl might do something he would later regret. Quickly, she summoned Eva.

"Is what Vinell do, now?" was Eva's first question.

"Is not so much what she do as what somebody do to her," Daisy answered.

"What? Earl beat her again? But you know I don't have any problem wid dat! If him was beatin' her bottom long time she wouldn't-"

"Poor Earl," Daisy interrupted. "You daughter pregnant, Miss Eva."

Eva barely batted an eyelid. It was as though she was expecting it, Daisy thought. After a few seconds she asked, "She tell you who is di father?"

"She tell me last night dat it was a boy who come wid one crusade to Elfin, few months ago."

"But him mus' gone long time!" Eva exclaimed.

"Yes, but Earl report it to di police because Vinell is under age," Daisy told her. "When dem find dat boy, is prison him goin' for sure!"

The two women decided that night, that it was time for Vinell to return home. Daisy made Eva promise to treat her gently, telling her how helpful the girl had been while she lived with them.

A few weeks later, the police came to see Eva in Ingram. They had found the man accused of impregnating her daughter and now had him in custody. Vinell sheepishly identified him as the father of her unborn child and the case was over almost before it had begun. Eva had felt sorry for the young man as they led him away. Knowing Vinell, she felt sure that she was much more at fault than the poor fellow.

Earl did not share those feelings. He had sworn that if he only got the chance, he would have to "do something" to the man who could "take advantage" of his sister like that. Daisy and Eva warned him to stay away from the trial.

Thankfully, that was the same week that Peter Masters decided to make his entrance into the world. His mother had been in labor for many hours, before the doctors decided that a Caesarian section would have to be done. Complications had later set in and for days, Earl was unsure that the mother of his children would survive this ordeal.

By the time Daisy was finally out of danger, Dennis was safely confined within the walls of his prison cell, far away from whatever lingering malice Earl might still have held against him. So caught up had he been with his own problems, that he hadn't even had the time to see what Dennis Barton looked like.

Eva kept her promise to Daisy. She did her best for her daughter throughout the girl's pregnancy. It was comparatively easy, since Vinell was much more amenable in her present state. She had not, for many years, experienced such a tranquil existence with Vinell in the house. Eva attributed this to the fact that the condition of childbearing was causing her to mature, and she was actually looking forward to a quieter state of living with her daughter and new grandchild.

She had recently taken up sewing and was very proud of being able to provide for herself.

She could still remember the day she brought Pauline home. Vinell had disappeared and poor Earl was all over the place searching for her. It was she who had convinced him to leave that business alone and return to his own life. She knew how headstrong her daughter was and that if she did not wish to be found, nobody would find her.

When Daisy got to Ingram that evening, Eva and Pauline had just come home. She knocked at the gate and Pauline came out to see who was there. When she saw Daisy, she ran forward shouting excitedly, "Auntie Daisy, Auntie Daisy! Grandma, come quick! Auntie Daisy come!"

Daisy smiled broadly. She could never stop wondering how totally different this child was from her mother. She gave the little girl a hug as Eva came out of the house.

"What a excitement!" Eva said, grinning. "What a surprise! Why you didn't tell me say you comin', Daisy?"

Pauline had taken her bag.

"Is yesterday mi decide to come," Daisy answered.

"Go put down you auntie bag, Pauline," Eva told the child. Then to Daisy she said, "Somet'ing happen?"

"No," Daisy told her. "You worry too much, man!"

"Good. Come inside," Eva said.

Later that evening, after Pauline had been sent to bed, the two women sat together drinking mint tea. They could hear the wind howling through the branches of the trees.

"Rain might fall tonight," Daisy remarked.

"It definitely sound like it," Eva agreed. "Everybody at home a'right?"

"Yes. Dem children fine. Earl a'right too. Him big an' strong and stubborn as usual!"

"I know," Eva said. "Him still don't want get married. I goin' talk to him bout dat, again. I believe I kinda responsible for him attitude too."

Daisy knew it all too well but she wasn't about to broach that subject again.

"You still not hearin' from Vinell?" she asked Eva. "She don't get in touch wid you at all?"

"No Ma'am! But we a'right. As bad as it may sound, maybe we better off without her."

"I can't understand dat," Daisy replied. "How can a woman have no interest at all in her own child?"

"Me don't know, dear. Vinell is a different kinda person."

They sat in silence for a while. Then Daisy asked, "You ever meet Pauline daddy?"

"Not really. But I did see him at di courthouse."

"Him did come to Elfin wid a crusade, right?"

"Right. A preacher son."

"You rememba him name?" Daisy asked her.

"Of course, Dennis Barton."

Daisy coughed and sputtered loudly, as she choked on the mouthful of tea she had just taken.

Eva jumped up, slapped her helpfully on her back and said with concern, "You a'right? What happen? You a'right now, Daisy?"

Daisy coughed a few more times. She put the cup down and wiped her face.

Eva asked again, "You a'right, Daisy?"

Daisy nodded. Eva watched her apprehensively as she finished her tea in silence. She put down the cup and wiped her face.

"You look like you just see a ghost!" Eva remarked.

Daisy then said, "What if I was to tell you, dat Pauline daddy is in Elfin right now?"

It was Eva's time to be surprised. When she had recovered her voice, she said, "If dis is a joke it not funny at all, Daisy! Dat boy gone to prison long time an' I don't even know is which prison him gone."

"Him was in prison but him come out," Daisy informed her.

"Lord, have mercy!" Eva exclaimed. "You sure?"

"Sure, sure! An' him look lonely. Like a young man in need of a family. I believe him want to find him pickney."

After a minute Eva asked, "Earl know?"

"Him know di person, but him don't know say him is Vinell baby daddy."

"T'ank God fi dat!"

"But Earl not stupid, you know," Daisy continued. "I don't believe him would be carryin' a grudge for so long."

"I not too sure 'bout dat," Eva said.

"What good would it do him or anybody else, to go say him want fi attack Dennis Barton now?" Daisy asked.

"You could be right," Eva conceded. "Earl hot-temper but him don't fool."

"We have to find a way to tell him," Daisy said. "Pauline have a right to know her father."

"Yes," Eva agreed. "It would be a crime for her to grow fatherless like Vinell."

Then she got up from her chair.

"Maybe both of we could sleep on it an' try see what we could come up wid by mornin'," she suggested.

"You right," Daisy said, getting up too.

The rain had started. As the flashes of lightning brightened the room, Daisy thought briefly of her own family. She was sure they would be alright. She pulled the covers around her and began to think about Vinell again. Though she never would have told Eva so, she attributed much of Vinell's delinquency to her mother's attitude toward the girl. To herself, she repeated what she had so often heard Earl say, "Poor little Nelly!"

CHAPTER FIVE

Murder on Broadway

*I*t was on a night not unlike that one in Ingram, that Vinell first arrived in the town of Broadway. She had come in as a hitch-hiker. The elderly man who had picked her up warned her about the dangers of hitch-hiking. He told her the only reason he had stopped for her was that the rain was likely to come down at any minute.

She fed him the story that her mother and father were dead and that her stepfather had begun to molest her. She had no money and it was now necessary for her to go in search of a job.

The lies came easily when he asked her about her other relatives, and where she came from. But when he questioned her as to exactly where she was heading, he could tell from the hesitation in her voice that Vinell had no idea where she was going. Ned Forrester was quiet for some time after that. Then he asked her about her skills and qualifications.

She told him the truth, about having to leave school before time, though she left out the part about being a new mother. She would take any little job that would feed and clothe her, until she was able to finish her education, she said. It was then that Ned told her that he owned a business in Broadway and that he could offer her a job, if she wanted to work with him. Vinell was ecstatic.

When he took her home that night, his wife — Lela — was surprised but not overly so. She had long become used to her husband's picking up strays off the street and bringing them home.

The following Monday, Vinell became an employee in the grocery store which was owned by Ned and Lela Forrester. It was quite a large store. The sign above the door read:

NED AND LELA'S FOODS

She was enjoying her job. The couple treated her like the granddaughter they didn't have, taking time to help her appreciate values such as good morals and self-worth. About a week after her arrival, Lela took her shopping for clothes which she could wear to worship with them. She told Vinell they had grandchildren by their two sons who lived abroad, but that they only saw them about once or twice a year.

Vinell worked hard in the store, packing, wrapping, sweeping and cleaning. When they got home in the evenings, she insisted on cooking dinner for the elderly couple. They told her that she was working too hard but were as happy for having her, as she was for being with them.

Melvin Edwards worked in the grocery store too but mostly on weekends. He was one of the many strays picked up by Ned Forrester. Melvin told Vinell that Ned had found him when he had been strung out on drugs and hardly any use to himself or anybody else. Ned had known Melvin's father, now deceased, and had thought it his duty to rehabilitate and send him back to school. The two young people had hit it off from the first day they met.

Melvin was either working or studying and had little time for a social life. Vinell was not hugely worried by not being able to go out much.

The months and the years slipped quietly by, as she matured, gained confidence, and became a significant part of the lives of the Forresters. Lela suggested taking evening classes and improving her education, so she decided to brush up on what she might have missed out on at school. She wanted to avoid the embarrassment of looking foolish in her new class and to do well in her studies.

She had just left the library to go back home one evening, when she met Melvin in the street.

"Hi," they both said together.

"You know, you been running through my mind all day," he told her.

"Maybe dat is why I feel so tired!" Vinell said, doubling over with laughter at her own joke.

Melvin laughed with her, though not as hard. He was thinking that she was really a nice girl. Pretty, funny, hard-working and ambitious. He could make a life with her. Then he said, "Seriously though, you want to go see a stage show with me? Something nice goin' on uptown."

"What time?" Vinell asked.

Melvin looked at his watch.

"In exactly twenty-five minutes."

"What!" Vinell exclaimed. "You expect me to go home an' get ready so quick?"

"Why you think you need to go home to change? You look perfect to me."

"No, man!" Vinell protested.

"If you have to go home first, we not goin' catch it," Melvin said.

Vinell thought hard. Lela would be expecting her back soon. She chided herself for putting off buying a cell phone. Melvin did not have his. She would have to get a phone call someplace to let her parents – as she regarded them – know she would be home late tonight. She had not gone out socially for so long.

"A'right," she said finally. "I just goin' go in di library bathroom an' touch up mi makeup."

"You bring makeup to library!" Melvin said, with a laugh.

"Of course!" Vinell replied with mock annoyance. Then she ran off saying, "Don't move. I soon come back."

The two had a wonderful time that night. The show was great and they went for ice cream afterwards. Lela and Ned were perplexed over Vinell's absence. She had been too excited to remember to call home. When ten o'clock came, Ned decided he would have to try to find her. He drove slowly around the town, looking and asking if anybody had seen her. He got no word. After more than an hour, he decided to head back home. Maybe Vinell had returned by now.

He was passing the grocery store on his way back when he saw a light inside. The store had been closed from seven o'clock. One light was always left on in front, and one outside at the back. He decided to check things out. Maybe somebody had forgotten to turn a light off. When he went around to the back, he saw that a door was open. Something was definitely wrong. He tiptoed quietly in and saw the robbers, long before they saw him. He knew them.

Silently, Ned scolded himself about not calling the police instead of taking matters into his own hands. These were desperate criminals who knew him and they usually carried guns. He tried to get back out without catching their attention. It may have been his nervousness but just as he thought he was getting away, his left foot got caught under one of the shelves and everything on it came tumbling down.

Ned trembled in fear as the robbers approached him. He begged for mercy as the two men drew their weapons. He got none. They each put a bullet into him, before fleeing with what they had come for.

When Vinell got home, she apologized for not having called. She could see that Lela was upset. She told her how worried they had been and that Ned was still out looking for her. The atmosphere was tense as the two sat down to wait for the man they both loved.

Vinell had fallen asleep in the chair. Lela watched her resentfully for some minutes. Then she smiled. Poor Vinell! She was only a girl, trying so hard to take care of herself and everybody else. She had come into their lives like an unexpected puff of energy that had brought new vigor to their tired, though predictably pleasant lives. Then she wondered for the hundredth time what kind of people would allow this child to go off without finding and taking her back home. Well, their loss and carelessness was her and Ned's gain.

Lela had begun to nod off herself, when the doorbell rang. She jumped up and ran to the door.

"Ned!" she said excitedly opening the door. "Is you dat, Ned?"

It wasn't Ned who looked back at her when the door opened, and the instant she looked into Melvin's face, she knew that something was terribly wrong.

It was a huge funeral. Possibly the largest that was ever held in the town of Broadway. The morning was cool and damp after the showers of the night before. The simple, yet elegant little hall, stood on a corner lot close to the edge of the town. The gentle morning sun cast flowery shadows across the thick, green, carpet-like lawn that surrounded the building. There were many more people outside of the building than inside. Cars were backed up from one end of the street to the next, with a few spilling over into the main street.

The mood was somber. At most funerals, somebody usually found something appropriate to the occasion, to smile or even chuckle about. At Ned's funeral, most of those who were not completely overwhelmed by their grief, seemed to be hiding a smoldering anger behind their staid, dignified countenances.

Ned's older son, Elroy, was one of these. Vinell had met him and the younger son, Omar, a few days after Ned's death. They had both come home with their spouses and children. As she sat trying to focus on what the minister was saying about the resurrection hope, Vinell couldn't help remembering the night she and Lela got the news of Ned's passing.

She had awakened to see Lela opening the door for Melvin. He had taken Lela's hand to lead her back to her chair, but she pulled away from him demanding, "What happen to him, Melvin? Where is Ned?"

Melvin said nothing, but his silent tears told his story.

Lela's voice took on an unnatural quality as she repeated, "Tell me, Melvin! What happen to mi husband?"

"Him gone," Melvin sobbed, wiping his face with the back of his hand. "Criminal kill him, Miss Lela."

Vinell would forever remember Lela's reaction to the news. It was the most painful thing she had ever seen or heard, and she felt completely responsible for the woman's distress. She, herself, had not been able to shed a tear. It just didn't seem real. How could a sweet, kind, wonderful person like Ned be dead? A thing like this should never even be possible. For hours after Melvin had given Lela his answer, Vinell had kept repeating to herself, "Him gone? Gone where?"

Now, as she gazed at the expensive, beautiful casket, she knew it was real. She couldn't look at his dead face. Couldn't take the risk. Though he had told her that "the dead knows nothing", she feared this elderly man – who was the closest thing she had known to a father – would open his eyes if she went close to him, and scold her for not letting him know where she was the night he was murdered. Vinell would never be able to look at another casket without feeling afraid.

Elroy spoke to her after the funeral.

"We are taking my mother back to the States," he said.

"Oh," was all she could find to say.

"She needs us now," he continued. "She should be with what's left of her family."

Vinell nodded. Then she asked, "So what will happen to di store?"

"I am not exactly sure," Elroy answered. "You know it's closed now. Maybe we will find a buyer for it sometime soon."

"Oh."

"Mom doesn't blame you for what happened to my father," Elroy said next. Then he curled his lips and gazed at her. "I don't happen to share that opinion!"

Vinell looked at the floor.

I know you hate and blame me, she said in her mind. Out loud she said, "Sorry."

"Well, sorry cannot bring him back," Elroy said. Then he handed her an envelope. "Mom asked me to give you this."

Vinell took it without a word.

As he turned to leave, Elroy said, "We want you out of here by tomorrow."

That same evening, Vinell went in search of Melvin. She had not seen him at the funeral and wondered where he could be. She went to the house where she knew he had rented a room and knocked. After a few minutes, another occupant of the house heard her and looked out. Vinell asked her if she had seen Melvin. The woman answered that the young man was seldom there since his boss had died some weeks ago.

Vinell was puzzled. She thanked the woman and left. Melvin had been nowhere around during the days preceding the funeral either. The store had been closed, so where could he be? She had been walking about the town in search of him for the greater part of an hour, when she found him.

He was so stoned that he did not recognize her at first. Melvin was sitting on a wall with a spliff in his hand. His clothes were very dirty. They looked like the same clothes he had been wearing on the night of Ned's death. His surroundings reeked of stale urine and something else, which she could not name.

"Melvin," Vinell said. "What you doin' here? What happen to you?"

Melvin blew smoke through his nose. He leaned his head back and smiled blankly at her, but said nothing. He was about to take another drag.

"Melvin!" Vinell said urgently. "Talk to me, man!"

He paused then, with his hand in mid-air and looked hard at her.

"Vinell," he said, grinning broadly.

"Why you didn't come to di funeral? What happenin' to you?"

"I look like something happen to me?" Melvin spoke slowly, as though he was having a hard time finding one word to place behind the other.

"Is not you alone mournin' for Daddy Ned," Vinell told him. "You believe you feel worse dan me? I feel like it was all my fault."

"Is not your fault, man," Melvin said just as slowly. He took another drag.

"Listen, Melvin," Vinell continued. "I have to leave dat house by tomorrow and di store not goin' to open back. I want to know what you plan to do wid yourself."

"I can't tell you what I plan," Melvin answered. "I am happy now. That's what matters". He smiled.

"So you not goin' to continue wid you studies?" Vinell asked.

"Don't know. You worry too much, man. Tomorrow will take care of itself."

Vinell watched him in silence. She wasn't sure what to do.

"A'right," she said finally. "You want me to walk home wid you? You can decide you next move, tonight."

"Home?"Melvin said vacantly.

"Yes, home. You can't sleep here."

Melvin grinned and threw his head backwards.

"Birds have nests," he said. "Foxes have holes, but the Son of Man has nowhere to lay his head!"

It was easy to see that he was under the influence of a very powerful drug.

Vinell went closer to him and took his arm.

"Come," she urged him. "Come go home an' sleep off whatever you been smokin'."

He shook her off, though not unkindly.

"I don't ready yet, man. Is you should go home. It getting late."

She watched him for a few more minutes and then she left. It was clear that Ned's passing had caused Melvin to revert to his former habit of avoiding the harsh realities of life by using drugs.

She got back to the house shortly after dark. Vinell stood on the porch, listening to the voices of the children chattering and fighting among themselves. It didn't seem like the same house with this level of activity. And for the first time, she began to seriously wonder about her own child. She didn't even know her name, or what she looked like. Wherever she was, she hoped that her child was much happier than she was.

Timidly, she rang the doorbell. She had begun to feel like an outsider ever since the old couple's sons and their families had arrived. It was Lela who answered the door.

"Hi, Nell," she said. "Just the person I want to see."

She closed the door and followed Vinell to the room the girl had occupied, since she had come to live there.

"How you doing?" Lela asked, sitting on the bed. She motioned for Vinell to sit beside her.

"Not too bad," Vinell answered. "How are you?"

Lela put her hand to her face.

"Ah, mi dear," she sighed. "This is hard but life goes on. These things happen. You got the envelope from Elroy?"

"Yes."

"So you okay with that?"

"Oh," Vinell hesitated. "I didn't get to open it yet."

"Well open it now, man!"

Vinell reached under the pillow. Lela watched as she

pulled the flap and looked into the envelope. Her mouth fell open but no words came.

Lela smiled.

"Ned would have wanted you to have that and so do I."

"But...but," Vinell hesitated. "Why you giving me so much money? You always pay mi every week for working in di store."

"That is for your education, Vinell," Lela told her. "You still want to become a nurse, right?"

"Yes, but–"

"Just call it your inheritance," Lela told her. "Put it in a safe place. Open an account at the bank so you don't spend it all on shoes and clothes."

Vinell didn't know what to say next.

"And you mustn't blame yourself for what happened to Ned," Lela continued. "You didn't kill him. Those robbers did."

It was then that Vinell shed her first tear for Ned Forrester and all the good things that had come her way, through him and his wife. She cried for a long time as Lela held her close. When she got control of herself again, she thanked her benefactor and promised to use the money she had been given to improve herself academically.

"Why don't you go home, Vinell?" Lela asked. "I'm sure your folks must be missing you by now. Maybe things have changed."

Vinell shook her head. "I'm not ready yet," she said.

Lela saw that she could not persuade her to change her

mind, so she gave her a letter which contained directions to her brother's home. She cautioned her that her brother, Roger, did not live by the high standards her dead husband had. He owned a grocery store and a bar, however, and would be able to provide her with work and living accommodations. Then she hugged Vinell and bade her "Goodnight". They would say their last farewells the following day.

Vinell crept out of the house early the following morning, before anybody else was awake. She did not feel capable of facing the pain of the final parting with this woman who had been so good to her, and who was now suffering the loss of her husband largely because of her thoughtlessness.

She stood in the driveway and took one last look at the house. She thought again, as she had often done before, that this was the most protective house she had ever known. Its dark-red brick walls spoke of beauty, underpinned by strength. It definitely had a personality – kindly and serene, whatever the weather – with a transient little whisper that beckoned: *Come home!*

Resolutely, she wiped away a tear that was inching its way down her cheek and walked quickly to the center of the town, from where a bus would take her to her new home in Kenville.

CHAPTER SIX

The Daddy

*I*t was a cool, damp morning in Ingram when Eva, Daisy and Pauline sat down to breakfast. Eva had gotten up early to make a special meal of fried dumplings, steamed callaloo and chocolate tea, in honor of their guest.

"It nice, Grandma," Pauline said, smiling with approval as she chomped happily on the food.

"Glad you like it," her grandmother replied. "But you should know better than to talk wid you mout' so full."

"Sorry!" Pauline said, taking a bite out of another dumpling.

The two women smiled, watching her. They had not spoken since the night before. Eva sent Pauline off, so they could get a chance to do so in private.

"So you come up with anyt'ing?" she asked Daisy.

"You talking 'bout Pauline an' her daddy?"

Eva nodded.

"Not really," Daisy replied. Then after a pause she continued, "Sometime di best way to approach a t'ing like dis, is head on."

"What you mean?" Eva asked.

"Just tell Dennis dat Pauline is him daughta!"

"You could be right," Eva agreed. "But it goin' to be such a shock for her."

"Why? Is what you did tell her 'bout her daddy?"

"I tell her say him dead."

"What!"

"So is what I shoulda did tell her?" Eva asked defensively. "Dat her daddy in prison? How was I to know him would get out an' come lookin' for her?"

"It really goin' to be a shock," Daisy agreed. "Poor little girl! But she will get over it though. You goin' to have to explain to her dat you did make a mistake 'bout it."

"Yes," Eva said slowly. "I sure she will understand."

"So is what you did tell her 'bout Vinell?" Daisy continued. "I hope you didn't say she dead too!"

"No," Eva told her. "I tell her say her mother gone far, far away an' I not sure when she comin' back."

"Dat sound betta," Daisy said approvingly. "I feel sure say Vinell goin' to walk right through your gate one day when you least expect."

"If you say so!" Eva replied, doubtfully.

"I goin' home back today," Daisy said. "I will tell Dennis 'bout dis. Den we can arrange for dem to meet. How dat sound?"

"Sound a'right. I can't think of any other way an' Pauline deserve to know her dad."

"Okay," Daisy said, getting up. "We goin' do it like dat. Where Pauline gone?"

"Next door," Eva answered. "I goin' call her now."

Somewhere around that same time, Earl and his children were having breakfast, prepared by his daughter.

"When mom coming back?" Peter asked his father.

"I not exactly sure," Earl answered him. "Why?"

"I miss her cookin'," Peter said unhappily. Then he looked at his sister. "Why you won't pay attention when mom cookin', Winsome?"

The girl put her cup down and gazed resentfully at her brother. "If you don't want to eat, you don't have to," she said to him. "Nobody would miss you if you starve an' dead!"

"Winsome!" Earl scolded.

"Finding fault what him cannot fix!" Winsome fumed.

"I goin' learn to cook," Peter vowed.

"Please!" his sister shot back.

"I like your cookin', but some of di best chef in di world is man you know, Winnie," Earl said, trying to pour oil on troubled waters.

Winsome said nothing. Then after a while, "Men must learn to take care of themselves. I don't want to be any housewife!"

"So who would married to you?" Peter asked insultingly. "You can't cook anyt'ing for anybody to-"

"Shut you mout' an' eat you food, Peter," Earl said, before Winsome could answer.

Then he swallowed a mouthful and said to his daughter, "I hope I will be around to give you away, on your wedding day."

Winsome looked hard at him. She was not appeased. She got up from the table and began putting the emptied plates together. As she moved to the kitchen, she looked back and said, "Is your own wedding you should be thinking about, Dad. Not mine!"

Peter looked at his father and back into his plate. He took another mouthful and asked, "You believe mom coming back later today, Daddy?"

Daisy arrived home that evening. She hugged the children, then told Earl that she needed to speak to him, privately.

"Is what now?" Earl asked, when they were alone. "You plannin' to leave mi for good? We goin' get married, Daisy but-"

"I tired to hear dat!" Daisy said, cutting him off.

She felt almost sorry for him as she watched him with his head held low. Then he looked up.

"You goin' get a big surprise," he said.

"Really," Daisy said with heavy sarcasm. "Anyway, I have something more important to talk to you 'bout."

"More important dan we getting married?" Earl asked.

Daisy hissed her teeth.

"Me an' you getting married is fairy story," she told him. "This is real. We find Pauline daddy."

"What!"

Earl said little else as Daisy told him the story. She had made him promise not to overreact or become violent about what she was about to disclose to him. He was stunned by the news but managed to remain at least outwardly calm as Daisy spoke.

As he gazed vacantly into the silence, Daisy asked, "So?"

"So what?" Earl echoed. "What you expect me to do or say about dis now?"

Daisy cleared her throat before she spoke. "I was thinking say I coulda invite your madda an' niece here for di weekend. I would cook a nice Sunday dinna and we could invite Dennis."

Earl remained silent.

"What you think 'bout dat?" she asked him.

He stood up and looked down at her. Then he said somberly, "What a way you have dis whole t'ing plan out nice an' neat, eh!"

"So you don't believe them should meet?" Daisy asked.

"I don't know," Earl answered. He was clearly not pleased. "An' since you an' mum take over dis whole business a'ready, you two can just go on run it, man. I goin' for a walk."

"Rememba you promise!" Daisy shouted as he walked away.

Earl heard her but pretended like he had not. As he walked, he could feel his anger toward the man who had wronged his sister returning. He had always felt betrayed and insulted by what had happened to Vinell; like he had failed her. He had an urgent need to see this man.

He made his way quickly up the road to the tent site. The ushers had just started placing the chairs in place for the evening's service. From a distance, he could see Dennis fiddling with the sound system. He stood looking at him for some minutes, willing himself to stay calm. He didn't trust himself. Maybe he should allow Daisy and his mother to handle this whole thing. He was about to turn to go back, when Dennis came walking toward him.

"Hi, Mr. Masters," he said jovially.

Earl made no answer.

"I have never seen you here but you didn't want to miss our last night, eh?" Dennis continued. "Good for you, man. Better late than never, I always say."

Earl remained silent. He was sizing up Dennis. Their last encounter had not been pleasant but Dennis seemed to have forgotten all about that. Pauline must surely have inherited his expansiveness of nature from this man. It was like he didn't even know how to hold a grudge.

"You are early but that's okay," Dennis rattled on. "May I show you to a seat?"

"Is not church I come," Earl told him. His tone was ominous.

Dennis looked askance at him.

"Oh?" he enquired.

Earl was not sure what his next move should be. Abruptly, he reached into his pocket. Dennis watched him, curiously, as he thumbed through some pictures in the wallet he had taken out. Pictures of his children, Dennis assumed.

Then Earl held up Vinell's picture to his face and asked, "You ever see dis person before?"

Dennis edged closer for a better look. Then his heart leaped. His lips parted and he looked at Earl.

"You know her?" he asked. "You know where she is now?"

"I ask you first," Earl said tersely.

"Of course I know her!" Dennis said gleefully. "Shirley Templeton! Where is she, Mr. Masters? Tell me, please!"

"Shirley who?" Earl queried.

"Shirley Templeton! I am sure that's her!"

Earl cleared his throat.

"First of all, dis is not no Shirley Templeton."

"What? But-"

"Dis is Vinell Sarah Templeton," he said slowly.

Dennis nodded.

"Yes," he said. "Yes. That was the name I couldn't remember. The name I heard in court. So where is she?"

"I can't tell you where she is but I can definitely tell you who she is."

"Tell me," Dennis said quietly.

"My sista."

"Your sister!" Dennis echoed in disbelief.

Earl nodded slowly, not taking his eyes off him. Dennis

stepped back quickly, as though in fear. He seated himself heavily on an old chair, carelessly left in the yard, and looked cautiously up at Earl. He looked like a man in shock, looking down at his hands and back at Earl again, every few seconds or so.

"So…" he said hesitantly. "You have no idea where she is?"

"No," Earl told him. "But I know where her daughta is."

Dennis jumped back up. He looked foolish and Earl almost laughed. By this time, he had lost his first impulse to attack the younger man.

"Where?" he enquired. "Where is her daughter, Mr. Masters?"

"Why you want to know?" Earl goaded him.

"Well…" Dennis hesitated.

"Well, what?"

"Well, because…because her daughter is my daughter too."

Earl stood watching him, saying nothing.

"Could you at least tell me her name?" Dennis pleaded.

Earl looked hard at him. He was beginning to enjoy playing around with this man and wanted to keep jerking his chain for as long as he could.

"Please," Dennis said.

He told him then.

Dennis smiled, happily.

"Pauline," he repeated, as though to himself. "Pauline. Beautiful name. So when can I meet her?"

"You will have to ask Daisy 'bout dat," Earl said, tucking his wallet back into his pocket and moving away.

Dennis walked behind him.

"I can hardly believe this," he was saying. "Found at last. Now I have family. Thank you, Mr. Masters."

"Is Daisy you mus' t'ank," Earl muttered.

"May I come by later?" Dennis enquired.

"So you not preaching tonight?" Earl asked him.

"I should be," Dennis said uncertainly. "This is supposed to be our last night in Elfin."

"So come tomorrow, before you leave."

"Right!" Dennis said excitedly. "Early tomorrow! Please tell Miss Daisy to expect me. And thanks, again."

Earl nodded and stepped off the compound on to the road.

As he walked back home, he chided himself for letting Dennis off too lightly and quickly. He should have been harder on him, for the sake of his sister and niece. But it had been so hard to stay angry with Dennis. He was a very likeable fellow, he admitted reluctantly to himself. And Pauline deserved a good father. Maybe he would have to forget the past and accept the young man, if only for the sake of the child.

CHAPTER SEVEN
Roger Maitland

When Vinell first saw Roger Maitland, she knew – without having to be told – that he was Lela's brother. They had the same delicately sharp features and curly black hair. But Lela was small and slender, whereas this man was of medium height and weighed more than he should. He smiled when she came into the small cubicle that was his office, and asked her if she had a good journey.

She'd had to wait for hours for the bus, she told him. It had been slow going and when there were only a few more miles left to cover, the passengers were asked to disembark and change buses. The carburetor had conked out, the conductress told them. Vinell was tired and hungry when she got into Kenville at dusk. Roger ordered her a meal which she ate hungrily.

He had been expecting her, he said, and her living quarters were ready and waiting. Briefly, he bemoaned Ned's passing. Then he called somebody to show Vinell where she would be staying. When she asked about work, he dismissed that with a wave of his hand, telling her there would be more than enough time for that tomorrow.

Vinell walked up the stairs behind the young woman. Roger had introduced her as Jasmine. The building was old and the boards creaked as they walked. The first floor was where the haberdashery and Roger's office were. They reached the second floor and Jasmine took her down the passage to a door which she opened up. The room was small but seemed fairly comfortable. Vinell wondered if the other rooms she had just walked pass, were the same as this one.

She lay down on the little bed and fell asleep almost at once. She woke up suddenly in the night, and wondered where she was. Then she remembered. But where was that sound coming from? That must have been the sound that had woken her up. She listened. It was a woman, moaning. Vinell wondered who was with her. She hoped it wasn't Roger. Eva had warned her about Roger and his lax moral standards, but she did not expect to experience something like this on her very first night here!

The noises eventually stopped and she went back to sleep. When she was awakened a second time by a man hurling obscenities at somebody, whom she felt was too afraid to answer him, she closed her eyes and wondered what sort of place this was. When the sun rose against her window, she got up groggily. She had slept poorly and wondered if she would have to endure these night noises as a matter of course.

Jasmine knocked at her door at about seven o'clock. She showed her the kitchen and made her a cup of tea and a sandwich. Then she told her that she could get some food supplies at the supermarket up the street if she wanted to. Vinell went down to Roger's office about an hour later.

He smiled and asked her, "How did you sleep?"

Vinell looked down at her hands, remembering what she had heard the night before.

"Not well, I presume," Roger concluded.

She looked back at him.

"Is plenty people live upstairs?" she asked.

"Not really plenty," Roger answered. "Are you a Christian, Vinell?"

"Not yet, but I believe in God."

"Don't we all," Roger said without reverence. "So you are a little Miss Prim and Proper?"

"No. Not really."

Roger smiled, got out of his chair and perched himself on his desk, just inches away from her.

"You are a very attractive girl," he said.

She said nothing and he continued, "Lela spoke to me about a job for you. You could work in the haberdashery here and I have a bar down the road, too."

"You a big businessman," Vinell remarked.

He shrugged but she could see that he was pleased.

"But a pretty girl like you could earn a lot more for both you and me," he continued.

"How?" she enquired.

"By simply…" He paused as though searching for the right word. "By just entertaining."

"Entertaining?"

"You are a big girl, Vinell. You know what I mean."

Then she understood.

"You mean entertaining men?" Vinell asked.

He nodded.

She was shocked.

"So dat is what was goin' on upstairs last night," she said almost to herself.

Roger's expression changed.

"You will not do well in my world with that attitude," he warned.

"But I don't want to do dat!" Vinell exclaimed. "Anything but dat!"

Roger was obviously disappointed. He went back to his chair and watched her silently for a while. If he hadn't promised his sister to help her out, he would send this girl packing right now. But he felt sure that she would come around to his way of thinking, so he asked, "So you want to work at the bar?"

"I prefer to work at di store," Vinell answered. "It not much different from Daddy Ned store. I know how to do dis kinda work."

"Okay," Roger said. "Go and talk to Miss Audrey. She is the person in charge."

"Thanks," Vinell said, getting up.

Roger was still watching her. As she turned to go, he asked, "But you and I will get to know each other much better, right?"

But you more dan twice my age! Vinell said in her mind.

She could hear him chuckling, as she closed the door behind her.

By the end of her first fortnight in Kenville, Vinell had fitted quite nicely into her job and new home. She had asked to have a change of room to the other side of the house. She told Roger that the sunlight that came into the windows of her present room prevented her from sleeping late on Sundays. The real reason she desired the change – as Roger suspected – was to get as far as she could away from the whoring which went on in that place.

He told her he would "look into" her request.

It was when she went to the bank her first week there, that she met Mark. She wanted to deposit the money Lela had given to her, along with the rest of her savings. He was the person who handled new accounts and investments.

"Are you new in this town?" he had asked her.

"Yes," Vinell told him shyly.

"I see," Mark responded. "I am sure that a pretty young lady like you would not have escaped my notice!"

Vinell smiled.

"So where do you work?" he continued.

"Maitland Haberdashery," she said. "An' I live upstairs."

Mark paused, his pen in mid-air.

"You work for Roger Maitland?" he asked.

"Yes. You know him?"

His furrowed his brows. He didn't look happy.

"Yes," he told her. "I know him very well. He is my uncle."

"Small world," Vinell said.

"Is he treating you okay?"

"So far, yes," she told him. "I jus' start working dere dis week."

"Welcome to Kenville," Mark said.

He finished what he was doing and handed Vinell her passbook. Then he stood up.

"It was nice meeting you, Vinell," he said. "I hope we can keep in touch. May I give you a shout when I am passing down there?"

"Of course."

He came by the store one Saturday evening about a week later. They started dating not long after and Vinell was happy and comfortable. Mark was quite a catch. He was tall and dark with features not unlike Roger's, only thinner. Vinell liked his respectful manner and gentlemanly ways. She would cook him some good food and fatten him up when the time came, she told herself.

She worked hard and saved her money, and was pleased at how quickly her account was growing. Mark had given her the best investment deal the bank could offer. Roger took quite a cut out of her pay for rent, but the store did excellent business and the pay was good. Vinell was very frugal with what she earned. She told Mark of her intention to study, and asked him to check out some evening classes for her.

Roger was the only person in her life who made her uncomfortable sometimes. He always seemed to be in a bad mood, especially when Mark came by. He frequently ignored the young man or would acknowledge him grudgingly, before returning to his work. Vinell knew why. She had not only refused to let him pimp her out but she also kept repulsing his advances, though she knew this made him furious.

Time passed. Her relationship with Mark grew stronger as she learned to ignore whatever she did not like about her surroundings, and to enjoy what she could. By the summer of the following year, she had begun thinking seriously of moving out of Roger's place. She managed to locate a room, just a few chains away from the haberdashery. When she told this to her boss, she could see that he did not like the idea but she continued with her plans anyway.

It was the week before she was to move out that she returned from a date one night, to find Roger waiting at the foot of the stairs. Mark had just driven off. She could see that the boss was drunk.

"What you doin' here now, Mr. Roger?" she asked him.

"What a stupid question," he slurred. "This is my place!"

"But you not usually here at dis time."

"Is you I come to," Roger said, grinning foolishly as he moved closer to her.

Vinell stepped back. His intention was evident.

"You know that I like you," Roger said, still trying to get close to her.

Vinell kept dodging and moving as he lunged closer to her.

"Go on home please, Mr. Roger!" she pleaded.

She had run out of backing-up space and was now circling the floor, with the drunken man still after her.

"Is young boy you want," Roger complained, saliva drooling from one corner of his mouth. "What you believe Mark can do for you that I can't?"

"At least him don't smell bad like you!" Vinell shot back without thinking.

It was then that he grabbed her.

"You feisty little wretch!" he muttered, angrily. "Jus' wait 'til I finish with you tonight!"

Vinell screamed then. Over and over without stopping, and everybody in the building heard her. Roger had just pinned her to the floor when a man, dressed only in his shorts, came up behind them and pulled him off the frightened girl.

Another shouted from the stairs, "Let go di girl, man! You mad? Is rape you plan to rape her tonight?"

It was only then that Roger seemed to come to his senses. His hands fell helplessly to his sides and he moved away to sit tiredly down on a crate of empty bottles in a corner. His head and shoulders were stooped.

Vinell was still scared and crying when the man in the shorts said, "But look how dis big, ole man want rape off dis girl, eh? Him don't know say dat is a crime?"

"You must report it to the police," the man on the stairs told Vinell.

Jasmine, who was trying to calm Vinell, said quietly, "Is him a di boss."

"So because him a boss, him can do any wickedness him please!" the man in shorts said with sarcasm.

Roger got up then and, without a word, lumbered out through the door. They all heard when he started up his car and drove off.

The morning after was tight with tension. Jasmine had followed Vinell to her room to help settle her down. It was then that she told her that Vinell was the only girl who had come to work there, who had not yet slept with Roger.

"'Not yet!" Vinell echoed. "Not yet? Never!"

"Roger feel like him own every woman who work wid him," Jasmine said.

"Well, I am one woman him will never own!" Vinell declared.

"Is jealous him jealous o' Mark," Jasmine continued. "I wonder how him don't fire you yet."

"Him shoulda fire mi before," Vinell answered. "Cause if him try fire me now, is jail him goin' go for harassment an' attempted rape!"

Jasmine looked at her friend and smiled.

"You ah one tough little gal!" she declared.

Vinell then picked up a towel.

"Is bathe you goin' to bathe again?" Jasmine asked.

"Yes. I still don't feel clean yet."

"Well, I goin try get some sleep now," Jasmine told her. "But be careful how you deal wid di boss. Him can be very cruel."

"I can take care o' myself," Vinell said.

It was almost lunchtime when Miss Audrey told Vinell that Roger wanted to speak to her. She knocked and he bade her to come into his office. She had never before seen the boss in such a state. He looked awful. His eyes were red and he looked old and worn. He seemed to be having a terrible hangover. He motioned for her to sit and she faced him across his desk. Roger cleared his throat uncomfortably.

"Sorry about last night," he said abruptly. "Guess I got carried away. I don't usually behave like that."

Vinell said nothing.

"Can we forget about it and start over?" he asked.

She nodded.

"You are a good worker," he continued. "Miss Audrey speaks very highly of you."

"Thanks," Vinell said.

There was a pause before he asked, "You in love with Mark?"

"Maybe," she answered. The question was unexpected.

"And he loves you?"

Vinell wondered where this was leading.

"You have to ask him dat," she said.

"Maybe I will," Roger said. "You remember that room you asked me about? I'm giving it to you. It's much nicer than the one you now have and I'm sure you'll like it."

What was Roger up to? Vinell wondered. Out loud she asked, "Why?"

"Don't be so suspicious!" He chuckled. "No sensible businessman wants to lose a good worker. All I'm trying to do is make you feel comfortable here and forget about what happened last night. The money you would spend on rent should be used for settling down permanently with Mark, don't you think?"

"So I won't have to pay for dis new room?" she asked him.

"Only about half of what you are paying now. Call that an early wedding present from your boss!"

He seemed very pleased with himself. Vinell didn't know what to say. It sounded great but she was still suspicious.

"Go and check it out now," Roger told her. "Miss Audrey will give you the key."

As she got up to go, he said, "And what happened last night is all in the past now, right?"

She nodded and let herself out.

Roger sat staring unseeingly at the door, long after her had closed it. If Vinell thought she would humiliate him and get off that easy, she had a new thing coming! He chided himself for not sending her away long before now. But who could expect that a little thing like that would give him such a fight? Some women had what it took to drive a man to madness and this one definitely did. Look what she had made him do last night!

He couldn't understand what had come over him. Maybe he was losing his touch. Maybe she had made him wait too long. The others had been easy. But times were changing and nowadays women had their own ideas, and the law protected them too. He couldn't fire her now but no way would she remain in his employ, with this thing hanging over his head. That nonsense last night had given her a degree of power over him and he hated even the thought of that. She would never give in to him now. Stubborn little wretch! Well, there was more than one way to skin a cat!

He bent down, pulled out a drawer and rummaged about in it. He smiled when he found what he was looking for. It fitted neatly into the palm of his hand. It was a beautiful little trinket which could also give somebody the chills. He could not remember exactly where he had bought it. Somewhere in Asia maybe, when his now ex-wife was still his wife. She had said it was the scariest, most morbid thing she had ever seen. Yet, he could not help buying it – a small, intricately decorated box in the shape of a casket.

He clasped it between his palm and fingers and smiled again. He had known that it would prove useful one day.

He had remembered it while he lay sleepless in the earlier hours of the morning, wondering how to get back at Vinell Templeton for having made an ass of him. He had it all planned now. He replaced the trinket and decided that he would speak to his nephew, when the time was right.

CHAPTER EIGHT

Revenge

*W*ithin a few weeks of the night of the altercation, things had fallen back into place. In fact, they seemed to be even better than before. Her new room was as nice as Roger had described it; better even than the one she had been planning to move into. In this new location – a few feet away from the other rooms – she was no longer affected by anything distasteful that happened in the house. She was still wary of her boss and never let her guard down. But Roger seemed intent on doing everything he could to dispel any lingering doubts she might have.

He exhibited a pleasant, congenial side of him which Vinell had never seen before. His regret over what had happened between them that night seemed truly genuine – almost touching – and Vinell began to wonder if she had ever really known the man. He always acknowledged and was courteous to Mark whenever he came by. She was happy that he had finally accepted her boyfriend. Months passed and she became convinced that he was truly regretful of his past behavior.

Eventually, she completely forgave the boss and placed the unpleasant incident squarely in the past.

October had just stepped in and Mark had left town to do some specialized business at another branch of the bank, when Roger decided to throw a party in honor of Vinell and the other members of staff, whose birthdays he had forgotten that year. The party turned out great. There was more food than anybody could eat. The music and every-thing else was wonderful and the drinks flowed freely.

It was close to eleven o'clock when Andrew brought her a drink. They had been dancing together for most of the evening. She missed Mark but Andrew had done his best to fill in for him. He hardly left her side. He had been introduced to Vinell earlier that evening as Mark's first cousin who lived a few miles outside of Kenville. The resemblance between the two was uncanny. They could almost pass for twin brothers, though Andrew had told her that he was older than Mark by two years.

Vinell tasted the drink and made a face.

"Drink up!" Andrew encouraged. "This is a special drink for a special lady. It will make you feel good, I promise."

She drank. It did make her feel good. All nice and tingly all over. She smiled and thanked him.

"Want another?" he asked.

She nodded. He brought the second drink and this time, she downed it all in one gulp.

"Good girl!" Andrew said, with approval.

Vinell giggled and sat down abruptly.

"Not much of a drinker, are you?" he said, sitting down beside her.

They were sitting very close together and he put his arm around her. Normally, Vinell would have objected but she didn't feel like her normal self. She felt happier than she had thought it was possible for somebody to feel. The lights in the room, filled with cigarette smoke, looked like stars in a mistily, mysterious sky. Her whole body felt mellow and charged with desire.

Then the lights went dim and she was sitting on his lap. They kissed passionately in the shadows of the room. It felt like a dream from which she wanted never to wake up. Tonight, she would finally consummate her relationship with her love, Vinell thought blissfully, as he pulled her closer. Some minutes later, he held her hand and guided her out of the room to a more secluded spot.

She woke up in her own bed the morning after. She had no idea how she had gotten there. In her wobbly head, there were several blank spaces between the time she had taken that first drink and the present.

Resolutely, she smiled and told herself not to worry. The time she had spent with Mark had been as beautiful as she had always known it would be. She was happy they had waited. She knew that he loved her. He had told her so often enough. She tried to get up but lay quickly back down. Her head felt like a big stone was jumping about inside it. It was then that her eyes fell on the small package on the night stand.

Her heart leaped. Was it from Mark? Could it be…? No, she told herself. It couldn't be a ring box! That was too much to hope for. Yet Mark had been talking to her of the importance of marriage and family to him, though he hadn't actually proposed yet. She gazed at the package. It was beautifully wrapped and about the size of a ring box. She got up, more slowly this time, and reached for it. Then she pulled her hand back. She would take a bath first and calm herself a bit. Her head was still throbbing.

She was going into the bathroom when the phone rang. She turned back to answer it.

"Hello?"

"Vinell! How is my girl?" It was Mark.

"Fine. Thanks for di present, though I don't open it yet. You comin' over here later?"

"What you talking about?" Mark asked.

"Di present you leave on mi night table las' night," Vinell explained.

"I didn't give you any present last night," Mark said bluntly. "I am not even in Kenville, now. Don't you remember? You alright, Vinell?"

Silence.

"Talk to me, Nell!" Mark said urgently. "What's happening to you?"

"I soon call you back," she said, cutting him off.

He called back immediately after and she turned the phone off.

She leaned against the door. Yes, she remembered now but what was she to make of it? Mark was away. He had not been at the party. So who had she slept with last night? She felt confused. Slowly, she walked back to the bed and sat down. Then she took up the little package from the nightstand and opened it. What she saw made her gasp. It was beautiful, yet repulsive - an intricately decorated miniature casket.

Vinell's hand trembled and she dropped the thing on the bed. It was so creepy! She wondered where it had come from. Something strange was happening to her and it was nothing good. Hesitantly, she touched the box, opened it and quickly pulled her hand back. She half expected a tiny Ned Forrester to sit up and ask her why she had been so thoughtless on the night he met his death.

When nothing happened, she took a closer look. Inside was a neatly folded piece of paper. Gingerly, she pulled it out and read:

Vinell, Vinell, what will you do?
Andrew has AIDS, now so do YOU!
You wouldn't share your boss's bed,
So now you are as good as dead!

The sound Jasmine heard was unlike anything she had ever heard come from any living thing. She dropped everything and ran into the room. When she found her, Vinell was laying unconscious on the hard terrazzo tiles, at the foot of the bed. She was bleeding from a wound where her head had hit the floor.

Jasmine took her to the hospital. She remained her constant companion as Vinell floated in and out of consciousness. Mark arrived back in Kenville the day after, but he could get no explanation as to what had really happened from Vinell, even during her more lucid moments. Jasmine loyally remained tight-lipped.

After about two weeks, she was physically better and the restraints which had first been placed on her, were removed. But she was still eating almost nothing and had lost so much weight that she looked like a different person.

Vinell had had no time to bask in the false luxury of denial. It had all been too real to be denied. Jasmine found out that Andrew was indeed an AIDS carrier and the sex between them had been unprotected. But it was too early to have a conclusive blood test done.

She had cried more tears than she thought she had. She would have much preferred to be dead. Self-pity then turned into rage, and her only thought was to find a way to get back at Roger Maitland for what he had done to her.

Since he was nowhere in sight, she tried to take out her anger on anyone or anything she could lay her hands on, breaking and wrecking whatever she could. That was when the restraints were added.

She had given little thought to Andrew. As far as she was concerned, he had only been a tool used by Roger to hurt her.

"You not goin' talk to Mark?" Jasmine asked her one day.

She shook her head.

"Him dying to see you," Jasmine continued. "Maybe him would understan' if you tell him what happen di night a di party when-"

"No!"

And Jasmine never dared to raise that subject again. Vinell's mind − stricken as it was by pain and distress − had found a way to place much of the blame for what had happened to her on Mark. She did not think she would be of any use to him or any other man now, so she refused to see or speak to him.

It was Roger who told him how his girlfriend had chosen to sleep with his cousin, Andrew, as soon as he had left town. He left out the part of the story where he had provided Andrew with the drugs necessary to make Vinell give in to him, after engineering Mark's going out of town. Mark was not sure that he was getting the complete truth from Roger, but Vinell kept repelling any attention he tried to pay her, so he finally gave up.

At the end of her stay in hospital, Jasmine helped her move into Taylor House – a shelter for abused women and others like her, who simply had nowhere else to go. Vinell knew she could not go back to Roger's place, and she did not even have the strength to confront him about what he had done to her. Not that she had any intention of letting him get away with it. But the time for revenge was not yet.

She was still very thin, weak and afraid. Afraid of what the future might hold or even if there would ever be a future for her again. The tears still came too frequently, and she could never throw the feelings of helplessness, confusion, uncertainty and worthlessness. Frequently, she thought of suicide as a possible option.

But below, above and around all of this, floated the anger. It mingled, constant and unrelenting, with every part of her being. It simmered, smoldered, ebbed and flowed but it never quite went away.

She felt like a battered and beaten little kitten, caught in a merciless and worsening rainstorm. Eight of its lives may have already been spent but the ninth was refusing to go, furiously digging its sodden little heels in, if only to see what the spiteful weather would be coming with next. Her anger was her only fuel.

Vinell had been in Taylor House for almost a week before she started moving around a little. Quite a few of the other residents were HIV positive and most of those who had full-blown AIDS had sought refuge there, since they had been driven from their own families or communities.

Jasmine never stopped visiting her and they spent long hours discussing Roger Maitland, his business affairs, his employees and his wickedness. What Jasmine did not tell her friend, was that Mark now had a new girlfriend and that he was working at another bank outside of Kenville. Neither did she tell her that Andrew's health was fast declining and that he was likely to be dead sooner than later.

Vinell made a valuable friend in Tanya Cline. She was a slender, dark-skinned young woman who worked with the occupants of Taylor House.

"I'll be your counsellor for the duration of your stay here," Tanya told her. "I'll help you work your way through all the bad stuff that's been happening to you."

Vinell didn't even answer. She felt sure that this person could do nothing for her. *Nobody could!* But there was nothing else to do.

"You are Vinell, right?" the counsellor asked.

She nodded.

"And the last name?"

"Templeton," she told her.

Vinell watched disinterestedly as she scribbled something in a folder. Then Tanya looked up at her and smiled.

"You want to tell me a little about what happened, Vinell?" she asked.

That was the last thing she wanted to do. But the counsellor was used to that kind of reaction and Vinell was soon to begin regarding her as her saviour. Not that they had seen eye to eye at first. When she had first spoken to her about forgiving Roger, she flatly refused to hear it. But Tanya had stuck to her guns and before too long, Vinell began to have an entirely new perspective on life.

She came to understand that life with HIV could be full, happy and meaningful. Slowly, she was able to let go of resentment and hate, and in time came to experience the healing properties of forgiveness.

Finally, she opened up and told Tanya about the baby she had left behind. She had known for a long time that the child was in Eva's care. She had called her brother's house more than once and skillfully elicited the information she needed, from the unsuspecting Peter. Once, she had even dared to call her mother's house. A little girl answered and she felt sure it had been Pauline. Hearing the voice of the child she had abandoned had made her feel terribly guilty and she had never called again.

And this was the child whom she began to see as the pathway to her own future; the bright, shining little silver star, on which she would hitch her wagon which would take them both down that pathway.

She blossomed and improved and made plans. She could smile again, for there was hope. She started eating again and managed to regain some of the weight she had lost. She gave serious thought to Tanya's advice to study, in order to become a counsellor. She still had the money Lela had given her in the bank and for the first time in a long time, she began to think how best to use it. But she needed to see her daughter first. That was the most important thing now.

Four months passed and she decided to take the HIV test. She was not much fazed when she heard she had tested positive. The months of counselling had prepared her well for this. She cried a little but not like before. Then she hugged her friends and thanked them for the support they had given her.

Vinell went to the bank later that same day. She could hardly believe it, when she was told how much money she now had. It was quite a tidy sum and she withdrew it all and closed the account.

With a travelling bag and her money, Vinell headed back home to Elfin.

CHAPTER NINE
Full Circle

ennis turned up at the Masters' home the morning after Earl had gone to see him. Daisy had just sent the children off to school and Earl had also left out to go to work. He was barely holding his excitement in.

"Hi, Miss Daisy!" he greeted her cheerfully.

"Hi, Dennis. How are you?"

"Happy!" he answered, grinning.

She invited him in and told him what she could about his daughter and Vinell.

"I cannot believe it!" he had said over and over. "I cannot believe I have actually found them!"

"You don't quite find dem yet," Daisy corrected him, smiling.

"But now I'm sure I will," came Dennis' response. "When will you be having that dinner?"

"Next week Sunday evening."

"Great!" Dennis said, standing up. "I can hardly wait!"

"So where you heading, now?" Daisy asked.

"Back to the tent site. I will have to convince Frank to extend the crusade for at least another week."

"I like dat idea," Daisy said. "You need some time wid you daughta. You decide how you going to make her part of you life yet?"

"Not yet," Dennis answered. "But now that I have finally found her, I have no intention of letting her go."

"You goin' have to fight off her grandma to get her!" Daisy warned.

"Not at all, Miss Daisy! I owe that lady for taking care of my child for so long," Dennis said. "How could I just take her away? Something will work out. You'll see!"

"I feel so, too," Daisy said, showing him to the door.

He quickly made his way back to the tent and broke his exciting news to Frank Abrams.

"I have a daughter, Frank! Can you believe that?"

"Daughter?"

"Yes. I met her mother right here in Elfin years ago and now I am going to meet her!"

Abrams gazed at Dennis in silence.

"Well? Say something, man! Aren't you happy for me?"

"Back up a little," Abrams said. "Are you saying that you have a child, here in Elfin right now?"

"Not exactly. It's a long story."

So Dennis told him the story. Frank was amazed. He didn't know what to say. What he did know – almost for sure – was that the girl his young friend described as his daughter's mother, was the same girl he had forced himself on, in the shadows that night. He finally found the words to congratulate Dennis on his newfound relative and expressed the desire to meet her too.

When Dennis told him when and where he would be meeting Pauline, Abrams asked, "Do you think they would mind if I came along too?"

"I don't think so," Dennis told him. "That is a kind, hospitable family and they love people. I'll mention it to Miss Daisy just to make sure."

"Thanks."

Frank Abrams needed to see that child. He needed to know whether she looked anything like those he had left behind in the many towns they had toured, during the course of his ministry. He had never liked children and he resented the fact that he had to pay out money every month to feed their hungry mouths and keep those of their young mothers quiet. It was not a thing he was exactly proud of but he was quick to forgive himself for his many indiscretions. A man had to have his pleasures.

So he decided to use one stone to kill two birds: See if Dennis' daughter looked anything like his illegitimate brood and check out that nice young thing, in the person of Winsome Masters.

Early that Saturday morning, Daisy left for town. She was carrying the extra money Earl had given her, as well as her market basket and three scandal bags. Happily, she savored the excitement of what was to happen the following day. Eva and Pauline would be coming later that same Saturday. Her steps quickened as she approached the market. She had to get back in time to make a bigger than usual pot of soup to feed her own family, and her two visitors.

She got back home shortly after twelve o'clock and started the cooking. She was just about to add the seasoning, when she heard the knock at the gate.

"Dem come!" Peter shouted excitedly from the living room.

Winsome, who had been helping her mother, ran behind Peter out into the yard. Daisy peeped through the window and watched as her children took the bags and ushered Eva and Pauline into the house. She smiled and returned to what she was doing.

"Mi soon come," she called as she heard them come into the house. "Two ah you jus' make youself comfortable meanwhile!"

The family ate and chatted way into the night. Earl was delighted to have his whole family together.

It was almost ten o'clock when Daisy said, "Everybody to bed now! Church tomorrow, remember?"

Peter groaned.

"Him take after him daddy!" Daisy told Eva, looking challengingly at Earl, who refused to be goaded into saying anything.

Eva chuckled and got up.

"Come, Pauline," she said to her granddaughter. "Auntie Daisy putting us to sleep together."

The dinner and reunion turned out as beautifully as they had all hoped it would. The newfound father and daughter could hardly keep their eyes off each other. Daisy and Eva had cooked up a splendid meal of rice and peas and curry goat. There was carrot juice to wash it down, and for dessert, they had ice cream with slices of a special 'reunion cake', which Daisy had baked earlier that week.

Frank Abrams looked as happy as everybody else. He ate heartily and seemed to fit in perfectly. He dotingly watched the first meeting between Dennis and Pauline, as did the rest of the family but he spent much more time watching Winsome, who was seated opposite him at the table. The young girl met his gaze pleasantly. She smiled at him at first, but his gaze was getting to be a bit too intense and suggestive for comfort. She was just beginning to wish for an excuse to leave the table, when she felt his boot touch her calf.

Winsome sprang up from her chair, barely remembering to say "Excuse me", and walked quickly across the room, to where her father sat. Earl had chosen to have his meal sitting at a chair by the window. Frank grinned and looked away for a second or two, before continuing to leer at the girl. This was a sly one; playing hard to get! He felt lustful and excited. Boldly, he kept watching her.

The fork had been halfway to her father's mouth, when Winsome whispered something into his ear. Slowly, Earl put the fork back on his plate and looked up at the offender. If that look had been audible, it would have sounded like a war-cry.

Frank Abrams saw and understood the look and he choked noisily on the food he was about to swallow. Dennis slapped his friend on the back and he coughed some more. Everybody at the table had stopped eating. Daisy brought him water and he drank and sputtered again, before recovering. When he dared to look again at Earl, he was still watching him.

Frank then drank his carrot juice, but left before dessert was served. He expressed thanks for the meal and wished everyone well, but told them that he had to leave to do some preparations for the service that would be put on the following night. Then he smiled and walked away.

As the bus got closer to Elfin, Vinell became increasingly apprehensive. She was returning home after so long, without even having called to say so. All the concerns of the past months were replaced with worrying about how her relatives would receive her. She had considered going first to her mother's home in Ingram but had rejected that idea. She felt sure that she was much likely to get a better reception at her brother's house. Her niece and nephew – if nobody else – would be happy to see her, she knew.

As they sped past the open fields, spread out like an endless carpet of green velvet, Vinell briefly experienced the tranquility this sight had always given her. The cattle grazed as calmly as they always did, stopping only to raise their heads in acknowledgement of the vehicle passing. She chided herself for having taken the simplicity of that old life for granted. Vinell wondered whether she was likely to ever know such peace again.

She hugged the large bag on her lap, as if for comfort and reassurance. Then she opened her little handbag and smiled. At least she was not coming back empty-handed. This money would go a far way toward carving out a future for herself and her daughter. There were several ideas bouncing around in her head, but she had yet to set herself a positively defined course.

The bus stopped near the gate to the Masters' house and she got off. She stood for some minutes behind a clump of bushes on the roadside, watching the house. It looked better than she remembered but nobody was in sight. Maybe they were not even home. She wished with all her heart that she had not come.

But there was no going back now, so she walked hesitantly up to the gate. It was then that she saw the little girl running down the path that led up to the house, and instinctively she knew who the child was. Vinell wanted to run but her feet stayed fixed to the ground.

"Hi, Miss," Pauline said, smiling broadly. "You want to come inside?"

Vinell nodded, stiffly. She watched as the child opened the gate, wondering how that squalling baby she had run away from could have turned into such a beautiful little person. The feeling of guilt, with which she had become accustomed to living, was eclipsed by a rush of pride. She wanted to hug the child. To apologize. To explain. To ask to be forgiven. To tell her that she was the best thing to have happened to her.

Instead, she gazed numbly at her daughter as the latter led her up the path, shooting a barrage of questions at her:

"What's you name?"

"Where you comin' from?"

"Is who you come to?"

"Where you buy you pretty blouse?"

Despite the turmoil in her mind, Vinell noted with some amusement that her daughter was quite a little chatter-box.

Then came the moment she had so long been dreading. Pauline ran into the house, yelling, "Grandma! Auntie Daisy! Somebody come!"

"Who dat?" Daisy called.

"She name Vinell!" the child said.

"Vinell?"

The soap slid from Daisy's hand and she ran toward the living room. She stopped in the doorway, taking in the sight of Eva looking into the face of the girl they had not seen in so many years. Daisy felt this must surely be a mirage, so she closed her eyes and opened them again. Yes. There she was. Vinell, whom she had begun to doubt was even still alive. A little older, a little thinner, but looking more attractive and appealing than ever. Vinell, at last. Vinell!

What happened next could best be described as a jumbled, emotional torrent of surprise, disbelief, relief, laughter and tears. In all the years she had known her, this was the only time Vinell had ever seen her mother cry over her and it touched a part of her that had remained untouched for more than twenty years.

They hugged without words at first, just happy to be there together again. Happy that blood ties would keep them loving and needing one another, despite the bad times. There was no place for resentment, recrimination or blame. Daisy could not stop calling her name. Each time she tried to answer a question from either one, like:

"Where you was?" or "Why you didn't call?", she never got to, as the women started hugging and kissing her all over again. At one point, Vinell felt like she was about to be smothered, but it felt too good to tell them so. This was better than she could ever have dared to hope.

Pauline did not understand what was happening, so they explained it to her. This was her mother who had been compelled to go "very far away" when she was a baby, but who had now come back to be with her. And mother and daughter hugged for the first time.

Finding a mother and a father in the same week was quite a bit for little Pauline. She had questions which she was promised would all be answered in time. Her limited comprehension of the whole situation did little to temper her delight in knowing her mother. She worried that she might not be able to act in the right way to both her parents, but things soon fell naturally into place without much effort on the part of any member of the new-found family.

All this emotion was repeated when Earl came home later that evening. But he had questions that would not wait. He led Vinell onto the verandah, seated her on a chair and sat facing her.

"Lawd, I glad to see you!" he began. "If you ever know how bad I did miss you. What's been happening to you all dis time?"

Vinell sighed.

"Is a long story," she said.

"I have time," Earl said sitting back. "You know how many, many time I try to picture you an' what you doin' through all dis time? An' now you here. T'ank God!" he said, gleefully rubbing his large hands together. "I can't believe it. Little Nelly come back an' you lookin' so good."

Vinell smiled.

Earl assumed an air of mock sternness and said, "Speak up, little girl! Big brother want to know what you been up to all dis time. Why you didn't call, Nell? You mus' did know I would be worried 'bout you."

"Of course mi call," Vinell informed him. "But I make sure to call when you gone to work."

"What!"

111

"Yes," Vinell continued with a gleam in her eyes. "I call an' talk to Pete. I find out all what goin' on here from him. But him didn't know it was me."

Earl looked hard at his sister and shook his head.

"Well, dat tell me one t'ing," he said. "You don't change much; you still bad."

Vinell laughed.

"You not goin' tell mi even little bit o' di 'long story'?" he asked her.

She told him about life with the Forresters, Ned's death and moving to Kenville. She was careful to leave out all the negatives which had surrounded her sojourn in Roger's employ.

"So why you decide to come back now?" Earl asked.

"I miss mi big brother," Vinell said mischievously.

"But of course!" Earl said with an exaggerated self-importance."Everybody know dat!" Then he asked, more seriously, "But why you choose to come back just now?"

"Is time I get to know Pauline," Vinell answered.

"Dat sound right," Earl replied, smiling. "You goin' love her, Nell."

"I love her a'ready," Vinell said.

"You have any plans for you an' her?"

"Not really," she told him. "But I bring back a little money. Wi can make some plans round dat."

"You plannin' for Dennis, too?"

"Who?"

"Dennis Barton. Pauline daddy."

"Oh…" Vinell hesitated. "Mum was tellin' me 'bout how him meet Pauline few days ago."

"Yes, man. It was one nice big eatin', you see Nelly!"

"So him still in Elfin?"

Earl nodded.

"From him meet him daughta is like him don't want to leave her," he told his sister. "Him was askin' for you, too."

Vinell seemed lost in thought.

"You know what?" Earl continued as if inspired. "I believe both of you should come together an' plan somet'ing."

"So you an' him is frien' now?" Vinell asked, looking at Earl. "You don't want to beat him up again!"

Earl shook his head.

"We have to let di past go, Nell," he said thoughtfully. "An' him is a very nice person. Just like him daughta."

The two shared a comfortable silence for some minutes before Earl said, "Is like dis t'ing did plan."

"What?"

"Di way you an' Dennis leave dis place so long, goin' up, down an' all over di place. Den both of you just circle straight back to Elfin same time. What a somet'ing!"

Vinell nodded in agreement.

"Dinna ready!" Daisy yelled.

CHAPTER TEN
His Last Night

F rank Abrams sat gazing without seeing into the collection plate in his hand. It was late and the worshippers had gone home. Dennis had left for the Masters' home to visit with Vinell and their daughter. These days, he was almost always there. Abrams had heard that Eva had returned alone to Ingram.

There was hardly anything in the plate. The community had long had their fill of the oft repeated religious messages. The time to leave Elfin had come and gone. They should have left weeks ago but Dennis did not want to go. When he had shown him how little money they had collected a few nights ago, he had suggested quietly that Abrams should go on ahead without him, at least for the time being. But Abrams knew there was no point to his going on alone. He didn't want to begin losing money again.

A few coins slid from the plate to the ground. He watched them roll around in the dirt but didn't bother to pick them up. He was fidgeting in the chair, scratching at his paunch and grunting like an unhappy hog. He was no longer a young man and he had obligations. What would he do if Dennis decided to leave him altogether? Not for the first time, a picture of the gun he carried leaped to his mind. He quickly dismissed it. There had to be a better way out.

The coming of Pauline into Dennis' life had really thrown a spanner into the works. Then his eyes lit up in the darkness. Pauline! There could be something there. But what?

He would have to tread very carefully in order to avoid pushing Dennis away. He well knew that preaching was not the young man's favorite line of work. He was doing it because he had the natural knack for this sort of thing, as well as out of gratitude to him for having shown interest in him, while he was still in prison. He had begun to sense that Dennis was getting tired of being a preacher.

Abrams thought hard and long about how to get a solution to his money problems. He got his answer when Dennis told him a few days later that he had decided on quitting the ministry to set up a small business in Ingram. He had tried to dissuade him but Dennis quietly but firmly refused to change his mind. Then Abrams enquired as to where the funding for the project would be coming from.

"From Vinell," Dennis told him. "She and I will be going into business but she will provide the money."

Abrams smiled broadly and congratulated his friend on his new venture.

"I would so love to meet Vinell!" he said.

Meeting with Frank Abrams was the last thing Vinell wanted to do. To her, he was simply a shameful memory and she had more than enough of those. It was great to be surrounded by love and acceptance and she did not want to have that disturbed.

She was careful to take her medications on time as prescribed, but she didn't always succeed in hiding them from the rest of the family. When her mother saw her one day and enquired what the pills were for, she told her a story about having developed a bad stomach because of not eating on time.

"Is dat cause you to lose weight?" her mother asked.

"Yes, Mum."

"What you need is some good bush tea!" Eva declared. "I goin' to look some and put down so when you come home to Ingram I can boil dem for you."

Vinell thanked her mother as she watched her leave the room with Pauline in tow.

From the first day she had returned to Elfin, something told her that her instincts about her daughter's paternity had been right. But Pauline and Dennis had bonded so perfectly. The child was even closer to him than to her. Her present circumstance was such a blissfully dreamlike state, compared to all the turmoil she had endured, that Vinell

116

decided it would not be changed in any way by questions or doubt. Everything would work out fine, she told herself.

They had met again the day after she had returned to Elfin. She hadn't even known he was coming there that day. It was their daughter who had excitedly announced his arrival. Vinell, though curious, was hesitant to meet with Dennis Barton again after so long a time. She felt sure he would resent her in some way.

He didn't. To each of them, it was as though time had been put on pause. They stood sizing each other up; Vinell – timid and apprehensive, Dennis – joyful in disbelief. He hugged her as he would his sister and things just fell into place from that point on.

Dennis told her that his friend and mentor was desirous of meeting the mother of his child. He urged her to go but she kept putting it off. Then Peter brought her a note when he came home from school one day. It was from Frank Abrams and he was summoning her to "discuss a matter", which could affect her "negatively".

The note had been worded more like a threat than a request, and the old feelings of fear and uncertainty she had forgotten since coming back to Elfin, haunted her again. She decided to meet him, if only for her own peace of mind.

Evening was approaching, though the sun was still hot, when she got to the tent site. He greeted her pleasantly enough and offered her a seat under the shadow of one of the smaller tents. To Vinell, he looked old and worn.

"You look good," he said, eying her. "Though better to me when you were fatter. Still sexy, though!"

She didn't look at him.

"Is what you want to see me about?" she asked.

"Rush, rush, rush! Life is short, Vinell. Don't you think we should enjoy it?"

She said nothing.

"Remember that night, with you and me in the bush? I really enjoyed that."

"Is dat you call me out here 'bout?" Vinell asked him, irritably. "I was a child dat time. Di only reason dat nastiness did happen was because you was threatening to wake up my brother an' tell on mi. Dat was a shameful mistake that will never happen again!"

She turned to go.

"Nastiness!" Abrams echoed. "Is nastiness you call it? So how come something so shameful produce such a nice little girl like Pauline!"

Vinell did not think she was hearing right. She stopped in mid-stride and looked back at the man.

"What you say?" she asked. "What you talkin' about?"

"Dennis is not your daughter's father," he told her calmly.

"So? What dat have to do wid you?"

"Everything." Abrams slapped his chest with his hand and declared proudly: "I am her father!"

Not in her wildest dreams had Vinell considered that possibility. Though she doubted that Dennis was her daughter's father, the only other possible father Pauline could have, she felt sure, was a boy she had been friendly with shortly before she met Dennis. That person had since migrated to foreign parts.

"How you know?" She couldn't help asking.

"I have three other daughters and Pauline looks exactly like her sisters. Believe it or not, she is mine."

"Don't say dat again!" Vinell yelled, coming closer to him. "You too lie. Pauline is not yours. You dutty, stinking ole man!"

Then she grabbed him by his shirt and began punching and kicking him. The blows came fast and furious and Abrams was temporarily surprised by the attack. He put his hand up to his face and ducked. Then he managed to grab and pin both of Vinell's hands behind her.

She was helpless but still cursing at him and yelling.

"Let me go! Let me go, you dog!"

"Is you baby daddy you calling 'dog'?" Abrams teased.

She stomped on his foot when he said that, and he slapped her, hard.

She quieted down and he let go of her. She could feel him watching her. His touch, like his look, was still as revolting as the night she had first met him.

Then he said, "If you want to do a DNA test, I will pay for it."

It was at that moment Vinell became convinced that this hateful man was really the father of her child, and she began to cry. Quietly at first; then loudly and without care or control. Hard, wracking sobs that shook her body. It just wasn't fair. Look how much she had been through already! And now this. Her precious little girl had been fathered by this disgusting pervert!

Through her tears, she could see him watching her calmly, coldly and without sympathy. Vinell breathed hard and dried her tears. Life had to go on, she told herself. This was just another hurdle she had to get over. She still had her daughter to live for. She wiped her face and asked, "So what you goin' to do about it now?"

Abrams cleared his throat.

"No sense beating about the bush," he said. "I want you to convince Dennis to keep travelling with me and forget about settling down here. If you don't, I will tell him that I am his daughter's real father."

"What!"

"Yes," Abrams continued. "This is business, my dear. But if you have anything to give in exchange for my preacher boy, I am willing to negotiate."

"Anything like what?" she asked.

"Money."

"How you know say I have any money?"

"So what you and Dennis going to use to start up that business?"

"But dat money is mainly for Pauline," Vinell said.

"That's your choice, my dear," Abrams said. "I am sure that Pauline will be very happy when I tell her how you and I made her in the bushes that night, just minutes after you had sex with Dennis."

"You slimy, ugly, disgusting ole stinker!" Vinell spat.

"Sticks and stones, my dear," Abrams responded, nonchalantly. "Sticks and stones."

They glared at each other until Vinell turned away. She knew she was beaten. Franks Abrams definitely had the upper hand in this matter.

"How much you want?" she asked him.

He told her and she asked, "You goin' to take everyt'ing I have?" Her voice was almost breaking.

"I am a reasonable man," Abrams answered. "I could take less if you would be willing to throw in something else."

"What?"

"You."

She didn't sleep much that night. She told Pauline to sleep in another room since she wasn't feeling so well.

"What happen to you?" Daisy asked with concern.

"Nothing serious," she told her. "My time o' month, you know."

"Oh," Daisy said, believing the story. Then to Pauline: "Go sleep wid Winsome, man. From your mommy come you not paying her any mind again!"

"Is true," Winsome agreed.

"A'right," the child said. "Night, Mommy. Night, Auntie Daisy."

Vinell told her daughter and the others good night and closed her own door.

She sat on the bed with her face in her hands. Her head ached. What a mess!

How could she possibly allow somebody like Frank Abrams to become a part of her daughter's life? Her own life had been so negatively affected by the absence of her father. But having a father like that would be much worse than having no father at all. A man who would sleep with anything youthful and feminine, would think nothing of molesting his own child, she felt sure.

No. No way! Vinell thought, resolutely.

She was not sure whether or not to tell Dennis to go with Abrams. If she took care of herself, she could probably live quite a long time with HIV, but she could not be precisely sure how her health situation would turn out. Eva was not getting any younger and Earl and Daisy had their own children to care for. What if she should die after she had sent Dennis away? Pauline would not have a parent. Those two were good for each other and she could not deny that she was falling in love with him all over again.

And now that creep Abrams wanted her money! This was what she was planning to use to carve a future for herself and her child. Except for Pauline, that was all she had of value. But how could she, who had been so disgusted by the harlotry at Roger's place, bring herself to do something like that? How could she ignore what she had been taught by Ned and Lela?

For hours she agonized over what to do. By the early hours of the morning after, she had convinced herself that she just had to do it.

She had abandoned her daughter at birth and she now had the privilege of coming back into her life and using the money to help her. She had never had to change a diaper, or stay up when her baby cried at night. This was the least she could do. This was a sacrifice of herself she just had to make. This despicable act she was about to do, would be a sacrifice of atonement, for her cruel abandonment of her newborn.

But Abrams had literally asked for it and by all that was just, he was going to get it! She would fix him for good.

Vinell reached under her bed for her travelling bag. Then she reached in and took out the box. It still scared her sometimes but it had begun to take the shape of a weapon she could use, instead of one that was pointed at her. Jasmine had thoughtlessly packed it in with her things, when she had brought them to her from her room at Roger's place. She had flung it far across the room when she first came upon it. The little casket lay in the same spot on the floor for several days.

Then the day came when she found the nerve to pick it up. She had once seen something about voodoo on TV, and it had given her an idea. She began to build a very small effigy of Roger. It took time and effort and it was done very precisely. It took her mind off herself, and made her feel that at least she was doing something positive, to pay somebody back for what he had done to her. When she was done, it looked a lot like her enemy and she placed it inside the little box.

It became like therapy to her to jab common pins into the effigy, as she quietly cursed at Roger Maitland. She knew it was childish but it eased the pain somewhat. Hardly would Vinell have believed this would have any particular effect on the man she so hated.

Never would she have imagined, that the very first week she started sticking pins into the effigy, Roger would begin to develop a serious heart condition. Of course, she would have been happy to hear that he was ill. But like every normal-thinking person, Vinell would have attributed something like that to mere coincidence. Nothing to do with what she was doing to his effigy.

It probably wasn't.

But Frank Abrams was no effigy. He was a mean, cruel man and she would not let him hurt her child.

Vinell opened the little casket and took out the effigy. She hid it far below some clothes at the bottom of a drawer. Then she found a small piece of paper and wrote a note. She folded it neatly, placed it in the little casket and closed the lid. This too, she placed in the drawer. Then she turned out the light and went to bed. The words she had written kept spinning around in her head for hours:

Buy a box like this and put it down
You just get AIDS and will die very soon.

They met at a secret place a few miles out of Elfin.

"I know you just want to get this over with," Frank said as he opened the door to the dingy little room.

"You right 'bout dat," Vinell agreed.

"You bring the money?"

"Here," she said, shoving it at him.

He counted it, placed it in his pocket, and began to undress.

"You take protection?" Abrams asked. "I cannot afford to support any more children, you know."

Vinell nodded.

"I am on di pill," she lied.

Despite how much she had wanted to hurt this despicable man, she had to admit that it just was not in her. Not anymore. Tanya Cline had certainly done a job on her, Vinell thought. She had managed to purge her almost completely of her thirst for revenge and she almost resented her for it.

The day before, she had gone to a pharmacy outside of Elfin to try to find the right contraceptive device; one which would not be obvious to the male partner, but would effectively block the transmission of HIV. The pharmacist recommended the best one she knew and Vinell had bought it for this meeting with Abrams. With steely resignation, she turned off the light and got into bed with the man she so despised, for the sake of her child.

She had driven a hard bargain with him, over the price of her body. He had finally agreed to reduce the amount he had previously asked her for by half, if she would sleep with him. The man was crazy with lust, Vinell thought disparagingly. She never dreamed that somebody would pay so much for sex. No wonder Roger did such great business with pimping.

She did not want to pass her disease on to Abrams, but she could not resist the idea of giving him a fright. When he stopped to let her off a few yards from her gate, she handed him the little casket, beautifully wrapped as it was when she had first gotten it. She watched with amusement the delight on his face when she handed it to him. Vinell slammed the car door and he drove off.

Later that night, for the second time in her life, she began to wash Frank Abrams from herself.

Abrams retired to his quarters, very pleased with himself. He had killed two birds with a single stone: got some useful money and spent a memorable evening with a beautiful young woman.

Vinell was not as young as when he had met her years ago but still very nice. It was probably his deathly fear of STDs, coupled with his hatred of using condoms, that caused him to gravitate to very young women. He prided himself on managing not to have picked up any such disease despite his lecherous habits, and he was convinced the reason for this was that he always picked young women who were either virginal or very 'little used'.

The money he had received from Vinell wasn't really a lot but it would have to do. He would invest it together with the little he had managed to save, somewhere that he would get some good returns on it. Meanwhile, he would have to set up a church in a well-to-do neighborhood, with a flock he could fleece at will. He felt sure that things would work out fine.

He reached into his pocket for the money and the little gift came up with it. He grinned. He had forgotten about it. Vinell! Playing hard to get and all this time, she really did like him. Women! Always saying "no" when what they meant was "yes". He peeled off the wrapping and his smile faded. What kind of a joke was she trying to play? Then he opened the lid, took out the note and read it.

The little box fell from his hand as he sat heavily on the bed. He was trembling. So this was it. He — the big con man — had been conned by a girl. Now he knew why Vinell had lost weight. But how could he, a man of the cloth, live with something like this? He could never face every day for the rest of his life with such a terrible disease. What he had feared for so long had finally happened. And now that it had, he was ready. His had been a good life, Abrams told himself. No regrets.

He leaned over and took the gun that he carried for protection from his suitcase beside the bed. Calmly, he got up and turned off the light. Then he lay down on the bed in the darkness. Finally, Frank Abrams opened his mouth, inserted the barrel of the gun, and pulled the trigger.

The sound of the single shot resounded over the deserted common, like an audible salute to the end of one man's war against morality and decency.

CHAPTER ELEVEN

Secrets Uncovered

*T*he community of Elfin was in an uproar over the tragic passing of the Rev. Frank Abrams. Life stood still as they paused to ponder over the life that had been lost to them.

How, they wondered, could a man who taught the message of redemption, lose hope to the point where he was reduced to taking his own life? What demon could have visited his soul, while innocence slept, and needled him into doing such a dastardly thing? What would be the fate of the soul of him whose mission it had been to save the souls of others?

It was Dennis who found the body. He had come back late from the Masters' house the night before.

He had spent most of the evening with Pauline, as Earl watched television while Daisy worked around the house. Winsome and Peter had been busy with homework, so he was alone with his daughter for most of the evening. He had tried to take her by bus to her own school in Ingram, but she had missed a few days because of the distance and he was concerned about that. He was dying for them all to settle down in Ingram as Eva wanted.

He tucked her in and watched her sleep for close to two hours, before Vinell came in. She had gone to visit with an old friend with whom she had lost touch, she told him. They bade each other a quick good night and he walked across the common, back to the tent site.

He called out to Abrams when he got in but the light had gone out, so he assumed the other man had gone to bed. He woke up late the following morning and still his friend was nowhere in sight, so he went to check on him. He found Abrams' body on the bed.

He had summoned the police and a crowd had started to gather, when Dennis remembered the strange-looking trinket he had seen on the floor by the bed. He went back in, telling himself that maybe he should leave everything for the police to handle. His curiosity got the better of him, so he took it up.

He examined it closely, wondering what it could have to do with the death of his friend. It was unusual but looked innocent enough. He was about to put it back where he had found it, when his eyes fell on the little piece of paper. He picked it up and read it.

Quickly, Dennis pushed the note with the little box into his pocket and walked out. He was now sure that an assignation with some woman had led to Frank Abrams' taking his own life. There was no point to his leaving this piece of evidence there for all to see. It was bad enough that the man had died by his own hand. This little piece of information would only make his friend look worse in death.

This was a side of Frank he had not known about, though he had his suspicions. But he had shown him kindness and Dennis felt duty-bound to protect what was left of the preacher's reputation, especially since he could not now defend himself.

The funeral was a gloomy little affair. Dennis conducted the service and even from the pulpit, he noticed how numb and confused Vinell looked.

"Did you know Frank, well?" he asked her after the burial.

They were sitting on the back porch of the Masters' house. She shook her head, mumbling she hadn't.

"You don't seem like yourself," Dennis continued. "You sure you okay?"

She nodded.

She had not believed it, when she first heard that Frank Abrams had shot himself. She raced up the hill to the tent site, with Daisy and the children in tow. A crowd had already gathered and everybody was discussing the late preacher and his final, cowardly act. She tried to elbow her way closer in but couldn't. Then the police came, followed by the undertakers. Vinell gasped as she saw the latter emerge, carrying the body of the dead man, all wrapped up and tied to a litter.

The sight of it made her shudder. Frank Abrams was indeed dead, though this was not at all what she had expected him to do. She had simply wanted to give him a scare. Now he was gone, without knowing that he had not even been exposed to the deadly virus; at least not by her. She left long before the others and walked home alone.

She had assumed that the little casket had been taken by the police and that the note had gone unnoticed, and had been disposed of with the garbage. She sat very still and tried not to react when Dennis took it out of his pocket and asked her if she had ever seen anything like it before. She shook her head in denial, not daring to speak. Then he showed her the note.

"I didn't want the police to find it," he said. "Everybody would know what made Frank kill himself."

Vinell nodded. She watched as he placed the box on the little table between them, and ripped her note into tiny shreds. Then he rolled the pieces into a ball and threw it away.

"So what you goin' to do wid dis?" she asked, looking at the box.

"Don't know. You want it?"

She nodded.

"Really?" Dennis asked in surprise. "I hate it!"

"It look kinda...kinda different," Vinell explained haltingly.

"Okay. It's yours."

She took it to her room later that evening. Then she removed the little effigy of Roger from her drawer. Carefully, she removed the pins and placed it into the box again. Then she crept out of the house and walked down to the river.

This thing always carried with it pain, unhappiness and now death, she was thinking as she walked. She should have disposed of it a long time ago. She would have to live with her disease and she could not bring Frank Abrams back, but at least she could try to prevent any other bad thing from happening as a result of her association with this thing. It was like an omen and she did not need to have it following her around.

The moon glowed bright and peaceful as she stood on the flat, gray stones beside the river. She watched as the waters plunged and bubbled noisily, over and through whatever stood in their path. Vinell breathed deeply and smiled, fondly remembering the occasions on which Earl had taken her and Winsome here to fish, when her niece was still little more than a baby.

Then she looked at the little box in her hand. In one fluid motion, she flung it into the heaviest part of the river. She watched as it hit the water, bounce madly around with the torrent, and was carried quickly away downstream. She turned to go when it disappeared from view, wishing that the turmoil in her life would also disappear.

Not many months later, unknown to Vinell, men were lowering a much larger casket into the ground at the

Kenville Cemetery. It contained the body of the late Roger Maitland. He had succumbed to a heart condition.

"But what is man, eh?"

"Is what you preachin' 'bout now?" Earl asked Daisy.

He was lying beside her in bed. It was a Sunday morning and the sun had just begun to peep over the edges of the clouds.

"Is not preach I preachin'," Daisy said. "Is just dat Frank Abrams just run into mi mind."

"Oh. Forget 'bout dat now, man," Earl said. "It was a terrible t'ing to happen, even though I neva too like him. But neither you or anybody else can do anyt'ing 'bout it now."

Daisy nodded solemnly. "Is true but-"

"Shut you eye dem," Earl interrupted.

"What?"

"I say you mus' shut you eyes."

"Why?"

"Just do as mi tell you , Daisy man!"

"I have betta t'ings to do dan playing 'round wid you dis morning, you hear?" Daisy said, moving to get up.

He held on to her.

"Please, Daisy," Earl pleaded. "Jus' shut you eye dem an' hold out you han', man!"

She knew that tone. He was not trying to joke around. Obediently, she closed her eyes.

Again he asked her to hold out her hand. When she did, she felt him place something in it.

"A'right, open you eye now," Earl told her.

She opened them and her heart leaped.

"Is what dis?" she asked, feigning ignorance.

"Open di box!" Earl commanded.

She opened it slowly, looked at the ring and then back at Earl.

"Well? You like it?" he asked, grinning.

She nodded. She knew this would have to happen one day. But that did not, in any way, quell the surge of over-whelming joy that was charging through her body.

"So…so dis mean dat we finally getting married?"

Earl nodded gleefully. He could see that she was happy and he was very pleased with himself.

"Earl!" Daisy cried, reaching for him, as she brushed away a tear that was threatening to fall. He hugged her back.

"All you have to do now is set di wedding date," he said.

"I can't believe it," Daisy said, trying on her ring. "Finally!"

"You more dan deserve it, Daisy."

They cuddled close for some minutes, before Daisy asked, "So is what cause you to decide to do dis now?"

"Well, it shoulda happen long time, but is Dennis cause mi to finally make up my mind."

"Dennis?"

"Yes. Him ask me las' week if I would mind if him ask Vinell to married to him."

"What!"

Earl nodded.

"Maybe we could have a double wedding!"Daisy exclaimed.

Earl smiled broadly.

"So what you tell him?" Daisy asked.

"I tell him say dat would be okay by me."

"Right," Daisy agreed. "What a excitement! I did know long time say him in love wid her." Then she laughed.

"Is what?" Earl asked.

"So Dennis believe you could stop Vinell from married to him, if she really want to?" Daisy asked.

Earl joined in the laughter.

"Or like I could make her married to him, if she don't want to," he said.

Vinell heard them laughing but never thought for a moment that it had anything to do with her. She sat up in bed and closed her eyes. Her mind went back to the evening before.

What could she say to Dennis? Had she not been in love with him, it would have been easy for her to say "No". But she was. With every fiber of her being. She was deeply in love with Dennis Barton and wanted nothing more than to spend the rest of her life with him. Yet, when he asked her last night, she didn't know what to say.

How could she promise, before God, to love somebody to whom it would be quite possible for her to pass on her disease? And how could she add another lie to those she was already living?

Vinell sighed. When would these shadows be lifted from her life? Would she ever feel completely happy and free again? If only she could confide in somebody! Daisy, Earl, anybody. But she was too afraid to share her secrets. Afraid of being despised by the ones who loved her most.

The children were beside themselves with glee over the news of the impending wedding. Vinell was very happy for Daisy and briefly forgot her own troubles, in the excitement of the day.

"Dis long, long overdue," she said, admiring the engagement ring.

It was almost midday as the three lazed about the house, after a late breakfast. The youngsters had earlier been sent off to visit their grandmother in Ingram.

"Nutten neva happen before time," Earl said smugly, as he watched the two women.

"An' di time come, now!" Daisy said happily. "But don't you suppose to have some good news to tell too, Nell?"

"Me?"

"Good news 'bout you an' Dennis, she mean," Earl prompted.

"Oh." Vinell was not sure what next to say. She forced a smile. "Is Daisy day today," she said evasively. "We can talk 'bout dat later."

136

"So him don't pop di question yet?" Earl enquired.

Vinell did not answer and Daisy could feel the tension beginning to build. Abruptly she said, "You too inquisitive, Earl! Suppose she don't ready to tell wi 'bout dat yet?" Then she took Vinell's hand. "Come help me start dinna!"

Earl was thoughtful as he watched them go. His little sister did not look happy. He wondered what could be wrong. He did not wish to pry, but maybe he should have a talk with Dennis, he told himself. Whatever the problem was, he felt sure that it could easily be resolved. He yawned contentedly and was about to doze off into a little Sunday sleep, when he heard Vinell's voice from the kitchen.

"Don't touch it, Daisy! Please, please don't touch mi now!"

"But it bleedin' bad," he heard Daisy say. "Come mi wash it off an-"

"I tell you, don't touch mi!" Vinell shouted again.

Earl ran toward the kitchen.

"Is what happenin' here?" he asked from the doorway.

"Vinell cut her han' wid di knife while she was season-ing di meat," Daisy explained. "I trying to help her, but I don't know why she carrying on like dis!"

"But it bleedin'!" Earl said, reaching for his sister's hand.

"Why di two o' you won't leave me alone, eh?" Vinell said, pulling away from him. "I can take care of myself!"

With that she pushed past her brother and rushed into the bathroom, leaving Earl and Daisy staring at each other in confusion.

"Is what happen to her?" Daisy asked, bewildered.

Earl shrugged.

"Maybe she just frighten," he said. "She soon a'right again."

But as Daisy turned back to the counter, Vinell ran past Earl back into the kitchen.

"Blood must be get on di meat, too," she said, peering into the bowl.

"Little mus' get on it, yes," Daisy agreed. "Don't worry 'bout dat, man. I soon wash it off."

"No!" Vinell shouted, grabbing up the bowl. "I can't take dat chance!" she said, heading for the door.

"So what you goin' do wid di meat?" Earl asked, blocking her way.

"I have to throw it away," she said, trying to push past him.

"Give me di pan an' go lie down till you feel betta," Earl said.

Vinell dodged as Earl reached for the bowl.

"Get out ah mi way, Earl!" she bellowed. " Trust me on dis, please! I have to throw it away."

"Why?" Earl asked her. "Why you feel you have to throw it away?"

"Because mi blood catch it."

"So what?" Earl asked her. "Daisy can take care o' dat easy."

"I can't take dat chance," Vinell repeated. "Get out o' mi way, man!"

Earl stood his ground.

"What chance, Nelly?" he asked. "What chance you talkin' 'bout?"

Silence.

"Something wrong wid you, Nell?" Daisy asked hesitantly. "Something wrong wid you blood? Is…is dat why you takin' so much tablet?"

Vinell's arms encircled the huge bowl, hugging it close to her chest. It was made from sturdy ceramic and contained about three pounds of raw meat, cut into small pieces. She held on to it as a sailor would to a lifeboat in a storm.

"You sick, Nelly?" Earl asked fearfully. "You sick, bad?"

It slid from her grasp then, breaking into several pieces as it hit the floor. The wedges of meat, thickly coated with seasoning, sloshed lazily around and among the broken pieces. Vinell gazed as though mesmerized at the mess on the floor. Earl and Daisy watched her in silence.

"Mi have HIV," she admitted, finally. "An' I don't want any o' you to catch it."

CHAPTER TWELVE
To the Future

*T*he family had fish for dinner instead, that evening. Only the children seemed to have much of an appetite. Peter ate his own portion as well as much of his father's. When they were all done, Daisy made them all wash up and go to bed. Then she and Earl sat down to hear Vinell's story.

Both were visibly stunned as she spoke, with very little interruption from either of them. She couldn't help shedding a few quiet tears of self-pity. Her brother's tears of rage over the hurt she had suffered, were more than her own. She could not remember ever seeing him cry. When her story ended, he hugged her close and promised to take care of her for the rest of both their lives.

"So what about Dennis now?" Daisy asked. "You goin' tell him?"

"I have to," Vinell replied.

"Everyt'ing?" Daisy pressed. "'Bout Pauline, too?"

Vinell nodded.

"Him deserve to know," she said.

"You right," Earl agreed. "But what about Pauline an' mum?"

"I don't believe she should tell any pickney 'bout dis yet," Daisy said. "Dem chat too much!"

"If we goin' to live in Ingram, I will have to tell mum," Vinell said. "But is Dennis is my problem right now."

"Him love you," Daisy said. "I believe him wi' understand."

"Pauline is my biggest worry," Vinell confessed. "I don't sure say him goin' still love her, when him hear him is not her real daddy."

"Dennis is a good man," Earl said. "But if him don't care 'bout her again, dat is fi him problem. Don't she was doin' a'right before him turn up? Don't worry yourself 'bout dat, Nell. You an' Pauline will always have a home here."

"Thanks," Vinell said, wiping her eyes.

"Just make sure you take care o' youself," he told her. "Visit doctor regular an' take you medication properly, right?"

Vinell smiled through her tears and said, "Right, Daddy."

Dennis could find nothing to say after Vinell finished telling him her story. He could not pretend that he was not deeply affected by it. In a few short minutes, she had shorn him of the blood rights to his daughter, of all the respect he ever had for Frank Abrams, as well as the possibility of having a future with her, whom he had loved for so long.

"So dat is it," Vinell concluded. "Now you know why I couldn't ansa you 'bout dat married business."

He nodded, dazed.

"But you can still see Pauline whenever you want to," she continued. "To her, you still her daddy."

"You tell her any of what you just told me?" Dennis asked.

She shook her head.

"I don't believe she ready for dis kinda news yet,"she told him.

Dennis nodded in agreement. They sat in silence for a few minutes more, before Vinell asked, "So you still goin' to want to start up dat little business in Ingram?"

"Can't answer that now," Dennis said, getting up. "I have to think about it some more."

"Of course," Vinell agreed.

He thanked her for being honest with him and left.

Dennis sat watching the men taking the tents down. The money Abrams had left in their joint bank account coupled with that found in his quarters, had been just enough to cover the funeral expenses, and take care of whatever other debts there were to be settled. This was the end of his days as a crusader and he wasn't even sure what his next move would be. He sighed as his mind went back to Vinell and the story she had told him.

It certainly was a lot to swallow. It was very evident to him that she did not expect him to want to marry her now. And that was as to be expected. Binding himself to a woman who had something so deadly, would be a crazy thing to do. What chance would that give him of fathering his own children? Not that his not being Pauline's biological father made him feel any less close to her. Nothing could change how he felt about that little girl.

What bugged him most about the whole thing was Frank Abrams' involvement in it. It didn't even seem possible that such a person could be the natural father of somebody like Pauline. She was well rid of him, as far as Dennis was concerned. That man, whom he had looked up to and respected for so long, had really had him fooled. And all the while Frank had managed to give the impression that he was such a pious Christian! Hypocrite!

What a litany of troubles Vinell's life had been! No one person should have to suffer so much. And yet, she had managed to stay strong and had done all she could to protect others from the virus she carried.

She was a better person for what she had suffered. No longer the dizzy, empty-headed young girl he had fallen for, so many years ago. A woman like that, Dennis concluded, could face and conquer any challenge life could throw at her. She was an ally to be cultivated. Strong, beautiful, honest and selfless. All the qualities a man could hope for in a woman.

Listlessly, he began separating the things he would need, from those that had to be thrown away. Some old pictures were among them: His father – staid and serious; Frank Abrams – cocky and self-assured; himself as a boy, and his mother.

He paused and looked more closely at the woman he had been told had died giving birth to him. She was very pretty and wore an impish little smile. She didn't look at all like a religious person. More like a feisty young woman he knew. Like Vinell. He had often heard his father speak of her fondly as his "spontaneous, unpredictable Margaret".

"Preacha!" one of the men interrupted his musings. "We ready now."

Dennis looked up, reached for his wallet, and walked out into the yard.

"So you done wid di preachin' business now?" the man asked, as he handed him the money.

Dennis nodded.

"Why?" he enquired.

"To tell the truth," he told him, "that wasn't really my thing." The man looked at him, perturbed.

"So you don't believe in God no more?" he asked.

"Of course," Dennis replied. "I just don't want to preach for a living."

"Oh." The man seemed placated. "Cause dat ole man killin' off himself shouldn't change anyt'ing for you," he continued. "People change but God don't change, you know!"

"True."

"Maybe is senile dat man get senile, you know, Preacha."

"Maybe."

The man shook his head thoughtfully.

"An' even though him do so such a wicked t'ing, I still believe say him can get forgiveness," he opined.

"Now that is something to think about," Dennis said slowly.

"An' I have more respec' fi a man who kill himself, dan one who murder somebody else," the man declared. "Although him wrong fi do it, is fi him life."

Dennis gazed at the man, thinking that regardless of how strange his words might seem, there was something to them.

"We mus' learn to forgive an' don't waste dis short life a condemn people," the man continued. "Dead can come to anybody, anytime. Is only God can't dead, and Him don't reject nobody!"

Dennis gazed thoughtfully at him.

"So who is the preacher now?" he asked him, smiling.

They shook hands and he told him to drive safely. When the truck had disappeared from view, he went back to what he had been doing.

He took up his mother's picture and placed it among his own things. Maybe he had inherited a little of her craziness, he thought wryly. He had made up his mind. He smiled as he picked out the clothes he would wear to visit and discuss his future with Vinell Templeton that evening.

The wedding was a splendid affair — the biggest and best Elfin had seen in years. The couple solemnly took their vows, as their friends and relatives listened and shared their joy. Then followed the outdoor reception, where the bride and groom were toasted and showered with good wishes. There was food in abundance and the wine flowed freely. The children, especially, had the time of their lives.

But though the joining together of Earl and his Daisy in holy wedlock was such a wonderful and memorable occasion, it had not turned out to be the double wedding they had hoped for. Dennis proposed again, but Vinell told him no.

"Why not?" he enquired.

"You know what you askin'?" Vinell said. "I really don't believe you know di risk you would be takin'."

"I know the possibility exists that I could get it but–"

"But nothing, Dennis!" Vinell retorted. "It would be downright stupid for you to marry somebody wid my problem."

Dennis was quiet for some seconds before he said, "But I love you, Vinell. I think if we are careful, it could work."

"Maybe it could work, an' maybe you could get it an' maybe both of us dead, leave Pauline!"

When Dennis said nothing, she continued, "I love you, too, but one of us have to t'ink straight. I want you to live your life to di full. Have a son. Not tie down youself to a sick person."

"I don't think of it like that," Dennis disagreed. "And what's going to happen to you now? You are still young."

146

Vinell smiled.

"You don't have to feel sorry fo' me, you know," she said. "You don't see how good I lookin'? An' I feel just as good. Is like from I tell you, Earl an' Daisy all dem secrets I was keeping, a dark, gloomy shadow jus' lift off mi! I neva feel so good in a long, long time."

He watched her, fully agreeing that she did look great. She had an exhilarating, infectious cheerfulness about her. Her cheeks had a new plumpness to them and the vibrancy of good health seemed to be bouncing off her skin. Yes, Vinell was still the most beautiful woman he had ever seen and he still wanted her. Permanently.

He had spoken to a counsellor two days ago, who told him that marrying a person with HIV would be quite a challenge but that it was "doable". He was not about to give up but gave in for the moment.

"So what you planning to do with yourself now?" he asked her.

"Well, you know I always plan on studying, right?"

Dennis nodded.

"I planning to get a little day job somewhere in Elfin, an' go classes in di evenings."

"Sound like a good plan for now. But you not planning to stay alone for the rest of your life?"Dennis asked.

"Maybe I could find a boyfriend who have HIV a'ready," Vinell said, laughing.

She was trying to lighten the moment, but Dennis did not find that funny.

"So you did t'ink about goin' to Ingram?" she asked him. "You still want to?"

He nodded.

Accepting the money from her to start up his business in Ingram, gave Dennis the opportunity to stay connected to Vinell and his daughter. He was to have a ready-made family and, for Dennis, that was like a dream come true. Pauline would be coming back with him, to her grandmother. Vinell and Eva had decided that would be best, since travelling all the way from Elfin to school in Ingram was beginning to impact negatively on the child. Besides, Eva was aching to have her grandchild back.

When her daughter told her about the virus she carried, Eva could not convince herself that she was not in a way responsible for that tragedy. She wished with all her heart that she could take it away from her and carry it herself. Since she could not, she vowed to do all she could to be the mother she ought to have been.

She helped Dennis find a suitable place for the shop and he stayed in one of the rooms in her house. It started out small, stocking everything from common pins to chicken meat. Largely because of the lack of competition in the area, the business grew and prospered beyond his wildest dreams. Soon, Dennis had to ask the owner of the building where the shop was housed to rent him more space.

He had a great relationship with Eva, who was overjoyed to have company in the house again. She simply took up where she had left off taking care of Pauline, and did Dennis' washing and cooking as well. She made it her duty to do all she could in influencing her friends and neighbors to spend their money with Dennis. Soon, he was a fully accepted part of the community and the trio was a happy little family. But Dennis still loved and longed for Vinell.

Since she did not work on weekends, she was able to come to visit with them in Ingram sometimes. The long talks she had with Dennis inevitably came around to the subject of their relationship. He told her about a counsellor he had spoken to regarding the possibility of their having a more meaningful life together.

"Other couples in our situation have done it," he told her.

"You still see both of us as a couple?" Vinell asked.

"Of course!"

She smiled. He was such a nice guy.

"But that's not the point," Dennis continued. "I want you to visit that counsellor with me."

Again she told him, no.

Dennis bided his time, constantly keeping abreast of every item of news regarding recent discoveries in the treatment of HIV/AIDS and doing as much research on the topic as he was able to.

Many months passed and Pauline was doing well at school. She was very proud of how much her father was looked up to in the community. Vinell continued with her studies, and the young women of Ingram vied for the attentions of the handsome, young businessman who had taken up residence there. Vinell was 'jus' his baby mother', they figured. He exchanged words with them and gave advice when they asked him.

Eventually, he began going out with the one who was the most persistent of the lot. He allowed himself to be talked into going to a late show with her, one Saturday night. He was busy getting dressed for his date, when a medical documentary came up on the television screen.

Dennis' heart raced as he listened. Scientists had recently discovered a vaccine which was likely to have the potential of providing immunity against HIV.

Excitedly, he called Vinell.

"You watching channel twelve?" he asked her.

"No."

"Well, turn on and watch it!"

"Okay."

Vinell hung up but he called her back.

"You heard it, Vinell?"

"Yes, I hear it," Vinell replied. "Hopefully, if you take dat vaccine, you can't get what I have, right?"

"Right! Will you go visit the counsellor with me, now?"

"Of course, Dennis, of course. What a possibility!"

"Great possibility," he told her. "I will call Monday and make the appointment."

"Maybe dem soon fin' a cure for AIDS, too," Vinell said, hopefully.

"Maybe. Good night, my love."

His date was rather offended by how distracted Dennis seemed to be that night. It was quite an exciting show, but she frequently caught him drifting off into his own thoughts, a faint smile playing on his lips.

She wondered if she had a rival for his affections and decided this was the night she would convince him to take their relationship to the next level. But when she invited him to her place for a cozy little drink, he declined. He thanked her for showing him such a great time that night and apologized profusely for leading her on.

He had "a fiancée living in Elfin", Dennis told the irate young woman.